OUT OF THE ASHES

ASHEVILLE ARCANA #1

RACHEL LANGELLA

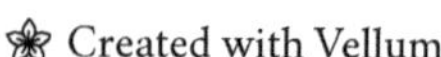 Created with Vellum

CONTENTS

CHAPTER 1

"Evening, Arden. You want the usual?"

Arden Gilmarin nodded at Gus, who both owned and tended bar at the Rainbow Room, Asheville's favorite watering hole among the gay supernatural community. No matter how tired or stressed he was, the atmosphere in the bar helped Arden relax and unwind. The alcohol didn't hurt either, of course, but Arden had wondered on more than one occasion if Gus paid someone in the local coven to keep a soothing charm on the place, since he'd never known of any fights in or around the bar, not even between factions of the community who didn't always get along under the best of circumstances.

Gus drew up a pint of a deep golden ale and passed it across the polished wood of the bar. "This one's called 'Waking the Dead,'" he said, then nodded toward the rear of the big, brightly colored room. "Your partner in crime is already here, in case you were wondering."

"Thanks, Gus." Arden picked up the frosty glass and took a small sip, then smiled in pleasure as the rich, yeasty brew tickled over his palate. "This one's a keeper, I think," he said.

He and his best friend, Whimsy Hickes, had a tradition of meeting at the bar on Wednesday nights to indulge in a pint or two—or more—of whatever local brew Gus had on tap. Asheville had a number of breweries, both magical and nonmagical, so there was always something new to try.

He glanced around the bar, nodding to the regular patrons he knew. But he didn't really want to get bogged down in socializing, so he took himself off to the rear booth where he and Whimsy usually sat. They liked to people watch, so they usually claimed a seat that commanded the best view of the room.

He could see Whimsy had already settled in, and he smiled as he slid into the opposite seat. "Hey, Whims. How's things? Blown up any cauldrons so far this week?"

"Very funny," Whimsy said, his dark eyes crinkling in amusement as he tossed his waist-length black hair back over his shoulder. It was glossy and sleek, and Arden knew from experience that it felt as soft as it looked. Whimsy had inherited his Cherokee mother's dark hair, eyes, and skin, but his unusual name and magical ability came from his father. "How was the meeting? Or maybe the better question is, how many of those are you going to need?" he asked, pointing to Arden's glass.

Arden huffed, but his annoyance had nothing at all to do with Whimsy. "A few, probably. The meeting was even worse than usual," he replied. As both a business owner in Asheville and a half-elf, Arden had been corralled into taking part in the informal "council" that oversaw the interactions between the various factions of the supernatural community. They were respected, even if their authority was limited. There were times when he wanted to flounce off in disgust at some of the inanity, but he felt compelled to stay as a voice of reason among the often fractious membership. "I simply can't believe how there can be so much squabbling over things that matter so little."

"The battles are never so heated as when the stakes are low," Whimsy said, offering Arden a sympathetic smile.

Arden rolled his eyes. "Unfortunately true. Would you believe that someone introduced a motion to adopt a leash law for *familiars*? Can you see us trying to tell the mages and witches they can't take their toad or rat for a walk without a leash?"

"Yeah, that's not happening," Whimsy said. "Percy wouldn't have put up with it." His last familiar, a gorgeous black cat, had died over a year ago, and he hadn't gotten another yet because he still missed Percy too much.

Arden smiled apologetically, reaching across the table to hold Whimsy's hand. "It definitely would have offended his dignity. But it gets worse, if you can believe it. There was also a motion to install waste bags in public parks in the supernatural neighborhoods for werewolves. The person who brought *that* up said it was the responsibility of people to pick up after themselves, no matter what form they're in."

Whimsy almost choked on his beer at that. After a brief bout of coughing, he stared at Arden incredulously. "How—? What—? They don't have opposable thumbs in that form! What are they supposed to do, leave a little flag and come back in the morning?"

Shrugging, Arden sipped from his glass. "Logic doesn't exactly figure in these kinds of discussions," he said. "When you get situations where the witches are yelling at the shapeshifters, or the Human Equality League starts in on their diatribe about 'incentivizing resettlement of supernaturals into normal communities in order to promote understanding,' it just all breaks down into chaos." He sighed. "As if that weren't enough, we're reconvening next week to hear from 'expert witnesses' on the subject. I didn't even know there *were* witnesses for poop."

"I don't see how you do it." Whimsy shook his head. "I sure couldn't."

"Sometimes I don't know how I can do it either," Arden replied. He frowned down at his mug of beer, tracing patterns in the condensation. "But someone has to, right? I mean, we do all have to get along somehow, and from time to time issues that are actually important get brought up. Like when we had to deal with that rogue vampire who was frightening humans, or helping put together the support system for orphan shape-shifters. The problem is that when there aren't real problems to deal with, the stupidity level goes up." He paused, smiling wryly. "Sometimes it makes me wish we had a real problem to deal with, like a demon or something, just so that people would work together instead of at cross-purposes."

"Be careful what you wish for," Whimsy said, wagging his forefinger at Arden. "You know words have power."

"You sound like my father." Arden raised a hand and made a warding gesture against the evil eye, a gesture picked up from his wizard sire. Not that he was any kind of a mage himself, but the habits of three centuries were hard to break. "But you're right. I don't really want a demon to show up. I just wish we weren't wasting time on idiocy instead of doing things that really mattered." He worried his lower lip between his teeth as he considered. "Maybe I should resign. I could spend the time planning another resort. Or at least having sex."

Whimsy studied him closely. "Is it the aftermath of a tedious meeting getting you down, or is something else going on? Divination isn't my thing, but I'm getting a vibe."

"A vibe? From me?" Arden shook his head. "You know

me, Whims. I'm the life of the party, right? It's probably just the meeting getting to me. Or the lack of big, buff supernaturals to lust over in the last couple of weeks. Even Julian is off on one of his periodic antisocial jags."

Julian Schaden was a vampire, and he and Arden had been "friends with benefits" for over a century before the term had been invented. After meeting Whimsy several years before, the three of them had become an informal ménage. There was no jealousy involved, since it was all just fun between friends, and no one minded if two of them hooked up without the third. It was safe and easy, and it meant that Arden usually didn't have to go looking for other partners if he felt lonely or horny. Still, he did like *looking* at newcomers, at least.

Whimsy sat up straight and flexed his bicep with a playful smile, but he wasn't that much taller than Arden, and while he was well-toned, his build was lean, not buff. He was also no more of a top than Arden.

"Maybe Julian will emerge from his funk soon," he said. "Or maybe someone from Tharn's pack will come to town."

"Maybe," Arden said, then shrugged again. "I'm not going to worry about it. Tonight is for us to drink and bemoan our dreary lives and dream of a brighter future, right?"

"Right!" Whimsy lifted his beer glass and held it out to Arden for a toast. "To good beer, buff men, and no meetings anytime soon."

"Now that's something I can drink to," Arden replied. He lifted his glass and clinked it against Whimsy's, telling himself to relax and enjoy the night. The Asheville supernatural community would take care of itself, just as it always had, and Arden would be right there with it, just as he had always been. This was his home, and every supernatural in the area was a part of an extended family. Like any family, they had their squabbles and their petty grievances, but when push came to shove, they always stuck together. It was, after all, the only way for all of them to survive.

CHAPTER 2

$\mathcal{E}$li Hammond stood just inside the meeting room of the Asheville paranormal council, listening while Tharn, the local werewolf pack alpha, argued to get Eli put on the meeting agenda. The room was cozy despite the October chill outside. The building they were in looked like a decrepit abandoned house, and the windows were boarded-up and blacked-out. But inside, the electricity and central heating were on, and the meeting room was furnished with an antique pine table surrounded by plenty of comfortable chairs, some of which were occupied by members of the council, most of whom looked bored already.

"The agenda is already set." The secretary of the council, an older wizard with a white beard and glasses, held up a piece of paper.

Tharn snatched it out of the wizard's hand and ripped it in half. "Then put him under new business," he growled, and the wizard's face grew pale.

"This is highly unorthodox. I'll have to check *Robert's Rules of Order...*"

Tharn glanced back at Eli and gave a little nod, but Eli

wasn't convinced anything would happen tonight, and he hadn't come all the way from Georgia to be stonewalled by bureaucracy. Eli drew himself up straight and stared down at the wizard from his six-foot-four-inch advantage.

"My pack was attacked. Some are dead. The rest are missing. How's that for unorthodox?"

Several of the council members gasped, and he had everyone's wide-eyed attention now.

"You gonna put him on the agenda now, Odell?" Tharn asked, folding his arms across his chest and staring at the wizard as well.

A handsome young elf with huge green eyes and shoulder-length brown hair held up his hand. "I haven't sponsored a new item in months. I'll make him my business if you're going to be anal about it, Odell," he said, his voice holding a tinge of anger. He turned his gaze on Eli, and Eli could read both sympathy and concern in his expression. He seemed to study Eli with unexpected intensity. "I am very sorry for your loss. Please, won't you take a seat and tell us what happened?"

Eli nodded his thanks to the elf and took a seat at the table. Tharn sat down next to him, and while it was sometimes awkward for two alphas to be in close quarters, Eli found Tharn's presence comforting right now. Tharn was older than Eli by a couple of centuries, and his craggy face was set in what seemed to be a permanent scowl, but his strength helped Eli feel more grounded. It helped, too, that according to Eli's pack chronicle, Tharn was a distant cousin, and Eli felt more comfortable asking for help from kin, no matter how many times removed.

"Under the circumstances, I believe we should dispense with the formal agenda and hear what our guest has to say." An older woman with a no-nonsense demeanor quelled

Odell with a withering look and a flash of fangs when he appeared about to object. "Please go ahead."

Eli glanced around the table and saw somber faces. Considering their collective numbers were small enough—no matter what type of supernatural being they were—any loss was a cause for sympathy and mourning. Likely everyone at that table was thinking about their own people and how easily it could be them.

"I'm Eli Hammond," he said. "My pack lives outside Clayton, Georgia. I went off on a trip by myself, and when I got back, there'd been a fight, and some of my pack were dead. The rest were gone. The scents of werewolves from another local pack were all over our settlement."

The elf spoke up again and leaned forward across the table. "I assume you tracked the other pack? Did they leave the area?"

Memories of the day he'd returned home to find his settlement empty and some of the buildings charred by fire rose up in Eli's mind. The scent of wood smoke and crisp autumn air tainted with the metallic tang of blood. Mangled bodies lying on blood-soaked leaves. Eli had dropped to his knees and howled out his shock, anger, and grief.

Fueled by rage, he had transformed and used his keener wolf senses to pick up the scent of the attackers. He discovered it was a familiar one: werewolf. The two local packs had met often enough that he recognized individual scents as well, and he could still follow the scent trail long enough to confirm it led back to the other pack's territory.

By that time, he'd cleared his head enough to realize he shouldn't barge into their territory alone. They had attacked his pack and killed five people—including a couple of his best fighters—so killing a lone target would be easy. Maybe they were even lying in wait, counting on him to seek revenge. As much as he wanted to assure himself that the rest of his pack was still alive, he couldn't risk going after them alone.

He'd returned home to bury the dead. Mortal law enforcement agencies didn't realize there were supernaturals in their midst, so calling on them, expecting them to treat this like a normal murder case, would only rack up more deaths. Instead, he went to Asheville, which not only had the biggest concentration of supernaturals in the Southeast, but it was also home to a pack with whom he could claim distant kinship. If he was going to find reinforcements to help him rescue his pack mates, it would be there.

"Yeah, I tracked them," he said, his voice low and rough. "But only so far. Didn't want to sign my own death warrant."

The elf nodded. "So you need help rescuing the survivors of your pack and getting justice," he said, seeming to understand the situation. He glanced around the table. "I believe our response to this should be obvious to everyone here. Am I correct?"

"Unprovoked aggression is worrisome," the older woman said, frowning slightly.

Odell scratched at his chin beneath his beard. "It is, it is. Very worrisome. But we can't afford to be hasty in our judgment."

The elf raised a brow. "Hasty? I would think senseless slaughter and kidnapping calls for an *extremely* hasty reaction!"

Another elf glanced at the younger one. This one was older, and he had actual streaks of silver in his golden hair. "Now, Arden, you are still young enough to want to rush into things...."

Arden turned to the older elf, scowling, and began to speak in the elven tongue, but it was obvious enough by his tone that he was angry. Other members of the council began arguing among themselves, debating the merits of getting involved. Odell seemed to be adamant that the situation was far outside their jurisdiction, while someone else claimed that if they were thinking of killing the killers, it made them no better than the murderers. Arden turned his attention away from the older elf and began to argue with a witch until Odell smacked his hand down sharply on the table, which caused everyone to stop talking and turn to him in surprise.

"It's obvious that we can't reach an agreement on this issue," he said, then looked at Eli. "I'm sorry, but we're going to have to take some time to consider this before deciding."

Eli clenched his fists as anger rose up, white and hot. With every minute that passed, the chances of his pack mates —his *family*—getting out unscathed diminished.

"Y'all take all the time you want," he said as he shoved back the chair and stood up. "We've shared the land for over a hundred years with nary a problem. I'm going to find out why a problem came up now."

Tharn stood up and swept a disgruntled look around the table before resting his hand on Eli's shoulder. "Let's go. There's nothing for you here."

Eli headed for the door without looking back. Tharn would likely help him, but the other pack was bigger than Eli's, maybe bigger than Tharn's, and if they were aggressive, he wasn't sure how a confrontation would go. Still, having Tharn on his side was better than being alone, and he intended to get his pack mates back, one way or another.

Tharn took him back to the forest where his pack made their home. In many ways it was just like Eli's, consisting of a cluster of simple wooden houses around a slightly larger building that served as a meeting place and storage for items the pack held in common. He called out for his second-in-command, Earl, and two of the younger werewolves before leading Eli to the meeting house.

They gathered around one of the tables, and Tharn's

mate, Morag, brought them all coffee before taking a place at the table. Tharn produced a large sheet of paper and markers and asked Eli to sketch out what he remembered of the settlement of the pack who had attacked his, and anything he could recall about the surrounding area.

Eli did the best he could, but it was clear the older werewolf was worried as he gazed at the paper. Tharn frown and rubbed at his beard.

"The way I see it, we either gotta sneak in and get the lay of the land or charge in full strength without knowing what we face. Either way, it's risky."

"If we can sneak in and find out where they've got my people, maybe we can get them free," Eli said. "We'll have more on our side then."

Assuming they weren't hurt or incapacitated, he thought. But he was determined to hold on to hope that his people were alive and would be well enough to fight their way out.

"We can take them. We're strong." Beau, a big man with red hair who probably wasn't even fifty yet, still seemed to have the cockiness of youth. "Let's just do it, Tharn!" Beside him, the other young werewolf, Jim Bob, nodded enthusiastically.

Without glancing away from the map, Tharn cuffed Beau upside his head none too gently. "Don't be a dern fool," he said mildly. "Or more than you can help, at any rate. Eli's pack couldn't take them out, so we gotta think this through. This ain't a game, boy, and if we fuck it up, they'll probably kill us *and* the rest of Eli's pack."

Beau looked suitably chastened, rubbing the side of his head, while Earl pointed to the community building Eli had indicated on the map. "I'd bet they've got them in a central place. Need fewer guards that way, and if they're tied up and gagged, they can't exactly plan an escape."

Tharn nodded slowly. "Makes sense." He glanced at Eli

and raised one shaggy gray brow. "Well, boy? What do you think? You're the only one here who knows the alpha of that pack. Think he'd keep them all together?"

"I think he'd have to," Eli said, placing his finger on the drawing of the settlement's large common hall. "We were twenty-five strong. They killed five of my people. They ain't got enough room for nineteen werewolves anywhere else or any other holding area that I know of. Seems like dividing everyone up would spread his manpower too thin."

"Not if they have access to magic, or keep them drugged up." A voice spoke up from the doorway, and Tharn snapped his head up, glaring at the newcomer. Then he relaxed slightly.

"I figured you might show up, Arden," he said, nodding a greeting. Eli immediately recognized the younger elf from the council meeting. "You ain't much like those fools on the rest of the council."

Arden smiled slightly. "I take that as a compliment," he replied, then looked at Eli. "May I join you?"

Eli hadn't paid much attention to Arden at the meeting, too angry at the council's dismissal to pay attention to individual members. But now he noticed that while most elves were tall and slender, this one was nearly a foot shorter than Eli, and he seemed boyish compared to most others.

"If you got ideas on how to get my people back, I'll hear them," he said.

"All right." Arden walked over to the table, moving to stand between Earl and Jim Bob. Earl reached out to ruffle Arden's hair, and Arden snorted and nudged him with a shoulder, hard enough that the big man actually had to take a step to keep his balance. Then he continued as though nothing had happened. "I have a couple of suggestions, at least. Like using magic to find out what's going on, without you guys running in there and getting yourselves killed."

"How are we gonna do that?" Eli asked, giving Arden a puzzled frown. "Ain't none of them witches or wizards on the council ready to help."

"Those idiots don't speak for all of us in Asheville," Arden replied, grimacing in obvious disgust. "They're complacent and self-centered because they've had peace for so long. I want to help you, and I have friends. I'm sure they will want to help you too."

"Can these friends use magic to rescue my pack?" Eli felt a surge of real hope, the first he'd felt since returning to find his pack mates dead or missing. He didn't know much about magic, but he'd heard about things like scrying and divination that could possibly locate them even from a distance.

"They can certainly try," Arden said. "If you'd like, I'll take you to them."

"You know these folks?" Eli turned to Tharn, looking for verification. If Tharn vouched for Arden's friends, then he wouldn't hesitate to accept the offer.

"Yeah, I do." Tharn gave a snort of amusement. "You, Whimsy, and Julian, right? The three of you been thick as thieves for a while. You hiring them out now?"

"They're my friends." Arden straightened to his full height. "Whimsy is a talented wizard, so I think he could help."

Tharn chuckled. "Don't get your back up, son, I was teasing you." He turned his gaze to Eli. "Arden's respected in Asheville, and he's got a lot of connections. If he says he'll help, then you can count on it."

Eli looked Arden up and down. Arden was pretty rather than handsome, with wide green eyes and a sensual mouth, and he had an open, guileless air that Eli was inclined to trust.

"Then I'll accept your help and be grateful for it," he said.

"All right." Arden smiled, then reached across the table,

holding out his hand. "I'm Arden Gilmarin, by the way. Or Arden Half-Elven of Gilorean and Marin, if you prefer the old form of address."

Earl laughed. "But we all know him as Sweet Cheeks," he drawled teasingly. "I'll leave which set of cheeks we mean to your imagination."

Eli snorted, but he wasn't surprised. Werewolves tended to be a lusty, bawdy lot. He hadn't heard of a werewolf carrying on with an elf before, though. He clasped Arden's hand—and he almost reeled back from the electric impact of the touch. His wolf rose and started growling a demand. Suddenly Earl's comment didn't seem so funny, and he wanted to punch that knowing smirk off Earl's face for talking about Arden that way.

For talking about his *mate* that way.

Aw, hell. He released Arden's hand quickly and stared at Arden with growing dismay.

Arden's eyes widened, as if he'd felt something in the contact of their hands as well. But then he frowned, seeming concerned. "Is something wrong? Are you all right?"

Beau and Jim Bob were looking back and forth between the two of them in confusion, but Earl and Morag blinked in obvious surprise. Tharn cackled. "Well, I'll be damned."

Eli couldn't tear his gaze away from Arden, wanting to wrap his arms around Arden and hold him close, to familiarize himself with Arden's scent. The wolf wanted to wallow in it. But this wasn't anything close to the best time for him to find his mate, and he wasn't ready to deal with it on top of everything else.

Swallowing hard, he glanced over at Tharn—and valiantly resisted glaring at Earl—and then looked at Arden again. "I'm okay."

Arden looked puzzled. He reluctantly pulled his hand back, then shook himself brusquely. "I can't imagine how horrible it's been for you, and, again, I'm very sorry for what you've suffered. But I can and will help you. If you want to come back with me, I can even arrange a place for you to stay while I round up the people I'm sure will be interested in assisting you."

"Go on with Arden," Tharn spoke up, nudging Eli pointedly. Obviously the old bastard had figured out what had happened and was pushing Eli to do something about it. "It might take some time to get everything in place before we can go get your pack back. Might as well stay with Arden while we do."

"What about my truck?" Eli asked. "My stuff?"

"I'll bring it to you tomorrow," Tharn replied, then waved a hand at them. "Go on, now."

"I'm taking him to the Riverside," Arden told Tharn. He smiled rather hesitantly at Eli. "If you're ready to go, that is."

Eli drew in a deep breath and rubbed the back of his head. He wasn't eager to go off alone with Arden, but he didn't have much choice. "I reckon I am."

"All right. Good night, everyone." With that, Arden turned and headed toward the door of the hall, opened it, and stepped out into the rays of the setting sun. Eli followed reluctantly behind.

"My car is just over there," Arden said, glancing up at Eli. He pointed to a silver convertible parked beneath one of the spreading oak trees. Arden gestured him toward the passenger side. "It's not locked," he said, opening the driver's door and slipping behind the wheel.

Eli preferred trucks with wide cabs that could accommodate his big frame, not sports cars that usually required him to attempt human origami to get in. Not to mention the sleek silver Mercedes SLK probably cost more than Eli's whole pack had put together. Most of them, including Eli, had jobs, but they lived off the grid and didn't indulge in expensive cars or gadgets. Hell, Eli still had a flip phone.

This is who you pick? Eli grumbled to the wolf, who simply whined at him until he folded himself into the car.

"The button on the side of the seat will make it go back so you won't be so cramped," Arden said as he pressed another button to start the car. Surprisingly, the engine didn't roar to life, merely gave a short rumble before settling into a subdued purr. Arden twisted the wheel, turned the car in a tight circle, and headed down the dirt road that led to the highway.

Eli felt around for the button and adjusted the seat to make more room for his long legs. The car looked like it handled well. He admitted—albeit grudgingly—the ride was smooth once they got on the paved road.

"I'm taking you to one of my resorts," Arden said, turning his attention from the road briefly to glance at Eli. Which was probably a good thing, since Arden drove at a speed that indicated he probably considered the normal speed limits to be merely guidelines. "It serves both humans and supernaturals, though there are wards between the two sections to discourage the humans from getting too curious. I should probably ask if you're worried about the other pack trying to hunt you down. If so, I can have Whimsy put up some additional protections for you."

"It wouldn't hurt," Eli said. He'd considered the possibility that the pack would try to find him, although there had been no signs of it so far. "I ain't one to take chances."

"That makes sense. Well, then, we'll take every precaution." Not slowing from his breakneck speed, Arden pulled a cell phone out of his pocket and dialed a number. "Hey, Whims. Are you busy? Can you meet me at the Riverside as soon as possible?" He waited, obviously listening to a reply. "Great, thanks. And if you don't mind, please call Julian and roust him out of his funk or sulk or whatever it is and bring him along. We have an issue to discuss. Promise him he can snack on me if he needs to, but get him there. Thanks, you're a treasure. Bye!"

Eli had to suppress a growl at the mention of this Julian snacking on Arden. He might not be ready to accept Arden as his mate, but that didn't mean he liked the thought of Arden being with someone else. He reminded himself sternly that it was none of his concern if Arden let a vampire feed on him.

Arden slipped the phone back into his pocket. "There, your protection will be taken care of in no time. Whimsy is an excellent mage, but if he doesn't think he can put up suffi-cient wards, we'll take you to Julian's house. He's had his whole place warded to the rafters."

"You're that sure your friends are willing to take in a stranger?" Eli asked, raising a questioning eyebrow.

"Yes. Is that so odd?" Arden turned to him again, offering a slight smile. "I'm willing to take you in, after all, and we've never met before. Besides, something tells me I'm *supposed* to help you. Call it a hunch, but I always follow my hunches, and they've yet to steer me wrong. Plus I've never seen an aura quite like yours before. I don't know what it means, but it means *something*. I know it."

Werewolves couldn't see auras like some supernaturals could, but Eli was familiar with the concept. He'd never been told his aura was unusual before, though, and he suspected he knew why his aura looked different to Arden.

"What's wrong with it?" he asked, trying to make the question sound casual.

"Not a thing," Arden replied quickly. "It's very bright and intense. Almost dazzling, really. I've never seen anyone who glows as brightly as you do. I'm shocked no one on the council commented on it. Odell at least should have been able to see it, even if the old coot is half-blind physically as well as morally."

"Maybe it was the lighting in the room," Eli said, wanting to steer Arden away from considering any other possibilities, such as a connection between them.

Arden laughed, the sound lilting and almost musical. "I take it you don't see auras? Obviously not, or you'd know that lighting doesn't make a difference. You'd be just as dazzling in the pitch-dark as you are in the sunlight."

Eli gave a little shrug. "As long as it's not bright enough to blind you and make you run off the road. Werewolves are tough, but not tough enough to survive a wreck at the speed you're going."

"Oh, I won't wreck. Elvish reflexes, you know. Don't worry, I wouldn't risk messing up that gorgeous face of yours. I happen to both admire and treasure great beauty."

"You said you ain't but half-elf," Eli pointed out, ignoring the way the wolf wriggled happily at the compliment.

"True. But my father is a wizard with a strong affinity for divination. That's why I can see auras, and why I trust my hunches." He smiled at Eli in a way that was obviously meant to be reassuring. "I'm more than just a pretty face, you know. I have talents of my own."

"Good to know."

Eli watched the scenery flash by without really seeing any of it. Whatever talent Arden inherited from his father hadn't revealed that Eli had recognized him as a mate. For once, Eli regretted not interacting more with other types of supernaturals or at least learning more about them. His knowledge of elves and wizards was lacking, but he didn't think either of them formed mate bonds the way werewolves did. If that was the case, then Arden could remain in ignorance, and Eli could go back to Georgia when this was over without an unwanted mate in tow. It was the best thing for both of them since they were different kinds, different people. Eli didn't want to relocate to Asheville, since it would mean either stepping down as alpha or moving his entire pack, and Arden seemed to have too many roots here to be enthusiastic about moving to rural Georgia.

Thinking about home made Eli's thoughts turn to the council meeting.

"I ain't out for blood," he said, thinking back to how some of the members seemed to assume he wanted revenge. "I always thought their pack leader, George, was a good guy. I just want to know why they did it, and I want them to pay for it. Ain't got to be by dying. Sometimes death ain't the worst thing to happen."

Imprisonment would be far worse for a werewolf. Werewolves possessed a deep affinity for nature and preferred to spend a great deal of time outside. To be enclosed in a small space like a warded cell would be hellish.

"I can imagine," Arden said quietly. "You need to be able to run free." Apparently Arden was following his train of thought without much difficulty. "We'll get your pack back, Eli, and the kidnappers will answer for what they've done." Arden's face hardened in determination.

"Damned right they will." Eli didn't bother to keep the growl out of his voice. Just because he didn't want to exact "an eye for an eye" justice didn't mean he wanted no part of the process.

Arden gave him a sideways glance, and there was no mistaking the heated gleam in his eyes for anything but awareness. "Remind me never to get on your bad side," he said, his tone a low purr.

Eli cleared his throat and looked away, trying to quell his own awareness of Arden's scent, his proximity, his charisma —everything making the wolf want to get closer. Arden was a pretty little thing, but Eli would be afraid of breaking him.

Eli always thought he'd find a strong, sturdy werewolf one day, not an itty-bitty half-elf.

"Ain't never a good idea to piss off a werewolf," he said at last.

"Pissing you off is the furthest thing from my mind. Trust me," Arden replied with a grin. "I'd much rather be friendly."

Eli didn't know what to say in response to that. His self-protective instincts were warning him to keep Arden at a safe distance, but he couldn't be rude to the person who was helping him either. He decided silence was the best option and kept his attention on the window.

Arden fell silent as well, and within a few minutes, they were passing quickly around the city of Asheville proper and off toward the north. Eli could see a wide, placid river on the left before the road swung away to the east. A small wooden sign appeared on their left, announcing "The Riverside," and Arden turned into a tree-lined drive that curved gently to the west. Eli felt a tingle of magic as they passed another sign pointing to "The Big House." A few moments later a building came into view.

Built of sturdy logs, it rose two stories with a wide front porch dotted with rocking chairs. Double doors with insets of stained glass were lit from within and depicted a deep blue river. Arden didn't drive toward the parking lot; instead he turned and parked in a spot marked "Reserved" right next to the porch.

"Here we are!" Arden said brightly. "My first resort, and my pride and joy."

Eli relaxed a little at the sight of the rustic resort. The trees and nature imagery helped him feel more at home than a sleek contemporary building would have.

"It's real nice," he said.

"Thank you!" Arden favored him with a wide, pleased

smile. "Come on inside. I can't wait to see what you think of the interior."

He led Eli up the steps and ushered him through the front doors and into a wood-paneled lobby. In the center of the room, a huge oak tree rose from beneath the floor, rising up through the room and disappearing through the roof two floors above. A wooden seat encircled the tree, and as Eli watched, a dryad peeped out from around the trunk and smiled at him. Eli waved at her, surprised but pleased to see a dryad in residence. He took it as a sign that the building and the grounds it sat on were deeply attuned to nature, which meant this was the perfect resort for a werewolf.

"How'd you pull that off?" he asked, nodding at the tree. There were normal humans milling around the lobby, so he didn't want to mention the dryad aloud, but he was curious why she'd agreed to move into the resort rather than staying in the wild.

"Oh, that's Aria. I've known her since I was a child and she was little more than a sapling. She's downright sociable for a dryad, so when I had the idea for the resort, I asked her if she would like to be the centerpiece of a beautiful building, and she agreed." Arden blew the dryad a kiss, and she blushed and ducked back around the tree.

"I'm surprised," Eli said. "I thought you'd have something real modern and shiny."

"Why would you think that?" Arden resumed walking, leading Eli off toward one side of the front desk.

"That car, for one thing." Eli followed along behind Arden, looking around as he did. "Your clothes, for another."

"Ah, externals. Don't be fooled by what you see on the outside, my big friend. The car is a hybrid and has a few magical enhancements—I can't run as fast as a vampire or fly like a witch or a mage, but in an emergency, I need to be able to get places fast." Arden opened a door marked "Manager" and gestured for Eli to enter. "As for the clothes, I'll admit to being a bit of a hedonist and liking things that feel good. Otherwise I might flaunt convention and go skyclad all the time."

Eli scowled as he walked into the office; he could have gone the rest of his life without that image in his head, especially since the wolf was perked up with interest. He quickly schooled his features into polite neutrality when he saw two men already inside. One had long black hair tied in a ponytail and dark brown eyes that studied Eli with keen interest.

The other man was almost as tall as Eli, and he moved with unnatural grace as he turned from his position near the window. He had brown hair that brushed the collar of his dark blue pullover, and his eyes were an intense blue. His scent immediately identified him to Eli as a vampire, even without the pallor underlying his olive-toned skin.

Unlike the myths the humans were so fond of, vampires could go out in the daylight, although they weren't anywhere close to as strong as they were at night. Demons were the creatures who shunned daylight, and most vampires didn't seem amused by the confusion between the two.

"Oh, good, you're both here!" Arden sounded pleased, and he moved to the smaller man, giving him a quick hug. "Thanks, Whims, I appreciate you coming. Eli, this is my dearest friend, Whimsy Hickes. Whimsy, Eli Hammond."

"Nice to meet you." Eli nodded politely to Whimsy, who was only two or three inches taller than Arden and shared his slender build. Eli might have thought they were related if he couldn't smell the magic all over Whimsy. This was the wizard, no doubt.

The vampire was eyeing Eli closely, and he didn't look away as Arden moved over to give him an enthusiastic hug. "Thanks for coming, Julian."

"Whimsy said you needed me, so I'm here," Julian replied,

his voice a smooth, rich baritone. He returned Arden's hug, then kept one arm around Arden's shoulders.

"I appreciate it. Julian, Eli. Eli, this is Julian Schaden. He has a lot of experience in dealing with rogue supernaturals."

The wolf pinned its ears back and growled at the sight of Julian staking a claim on Arden with that gesture, and Eli had to tamp it down. *Arden isn't yours*, he reminded it, but the wolf wasn't appeased.

"Mr. Schaden," he said, trying to sound as polite as possible while wrestling with a recalcitrant wolf.

"Julian, please." The vampire smiled at him, revealing a hint of fangs. "I assume you're the reason Arden had Whimsy roust me out of my self-imposed exile. What can we do for you?"

"My pack was attacked by another local pack while I was away," Eli said, careful not to allow his inner pain to show in front of these strangers. "Five of my pack mates were killed. The rest are missing. I need help rescuing them."

"From what Eli has told me, there wasn't any reason for the attack either. And if it's kidnapping, that doesn't make much sense. I've never heard of werewolves ever taking hostages," Arden added.

"No long-standing turf war that flared up?" Whimsy asked, offering Eli a sympathetic look.

"Ain't been any squabbles over land in my lifetime," Eli said.

Julian looked thoughtful. "Something must have set them off. Could they have come calling and someone got into a dominance battle?"

The "dominance battle gone wrong" idea hadn't occurred to Eli, and he gave it consideration before continuing. "I don't think it was a dominance battle. Our way was to look for a peaceable solution first. Dominance battles don't end in kidnapping, neither."

"Why don't we all sit down if we're going to discuss this?" Arden apparently had a strong need to play host, and he pointed toward a leather seating group on one side of the office. "I'll also get us drinks. Eli, what would you like?"

"Just water, thanks." Eli studied the grouping available seats before selecting what looked like the sturdiest piece, which was a wide chair with thick wooden legs.

"Certainly." Arden moved toward a small bar at the back of the office while Julian settled on the sofa. Whimsy sat down next to him. Arden returned shortly with a tray and handed Eli a large bottle of cold spring water before handing out a bottle of beer to Whimsy and a glass of deep red wine to Julian. He took a seat on Julian's other side with his own bottle of beer. "Okay, now we can continue."

Julian took a sip of the wine, then looked at Eli with a raised brow. "So if you don't think it was a dominance battle, do you have any theories at all? I just want to make sure we get anything relevant out in the open before we start figuring out how to proceed."

"Julian has done stuff like this before," Arden explained quickly. "He used to work with our local demon hunters, and he's trained a lot of young supernaturals in how to protect themselves."

"I ain't got any theories," Eli said, forcing himself to focus on the task at hand instead of how cozy the three of them looked on the couch. "I take a few days off every year. If I'd thought anything was coming, I'd have stayed home. We hadn't seen their pack in weeks, and we didn't have no problems the last time we did meet. This don't make a lick of sense to me."

"Hmmm...." Julian lapsed into a thoughtful silence, brow furrowed.

"I wonder if my father could help us," Arden said slowly.

He glanced at Whimsy. "You're the expert on magic, do you think it's worth paying him a visit?"

"Without any other concrete leads to work with, I think we should explore every option," Whimsy said, propping his arm on Julian's shoulder and leaning on him. "We can start with your dad, maybe see if he can recommend someone to do a scrying in the area where the attack occurred if he's not up to going himself."

"All right." Arden turned his gaze to Eli. "Tomorrow, I'll take you to see my father. He specializes in divination, but he's very old, so we try not to ask too much of him. Divinators are few and far between because it requires so much study and effort to get really good at it. Plus you have to have a knack for it. I could talk to the dryads in your woods, too, if you want to be around for that."

"Yeah, I do," Eli said, folding his arms across his chest. "I don't reckon it'll be easy to hear, but I need to know."

"I think it would be a good idea," Julian said. "Arden, you and Whims can take him to see your father, then go to see what the local dryads know."

"And what about you?" Arden asked, looking surprised. "You aren't coming with us?"

Julian shook his head. "Your father isn't wild about vampires, remember? And the dryads get unsettled by the undead. But something about this is bothering me, and I want to do some research, talk to a few people I know who might have heard something. We can meet back here tomorrow or the day after, perhaps. It might take a little digging, if you'll pardon the pun, to find what I think I'm remembering."

"Do *you* have a theory?" Eli asked, wondering if Julian knew or at least suspected more than he was telling.

"I have a bad feeling," Julian said, smiling sourly. "I've been around for a long time, and I'm paranoid as hell. There are few enough supernaturals in the world for it to be down-right frightening for one werewolf pack to abduct another for no reason at all. I want to make sure this is an isolated incident. How close are you to other packs? Would you have heard if this pack had maybe fought and killed off another pack entirely, especially if it was one in a different state?"

"Probably not," Eli said with a little shrug. "We're pretty isolated, and there ain't that many werewolves in Georgia to begin with."

Arden gave Julian a troubled look. "Are you sure you aren't just being more paranoid than usual, Julian? Remember, you were the one who thought that we were about to have a major demon incursion twenty years ago, and nothing happened."

"Yeah, yeah, rub it in, pointy ears," Julian said, ruffling Arden's hair. "I *hope* I'm being overly paranoid. I look forward to all of you laughing at me, okay?"

"I hope we all get to laugh at you," Whimsy said. "The alternative isn't something I want to think about."

"Trust me, being the one to always bring up the worst-case scenario isn't much fun," Julian said. He drained his wineglass and set it on the coffee table, then flowed grace-fully to his feet. "I'm going to get to it. I can travel faster at night."

Arden nodded and rose as well. "Be careful, okay?"

"Always." Julian leaned down and kissed Arden on the lips, not deeply, but not in a hurried fashion either. He straightened and smiled at Whimsy. "Come here, Whims, kiss me goodbye."

Whimsy stood up and slid his arms around Julian's waist, craning up for a lingering kiss of his own.

After a moment Julian pulled back and smacked Whimsy gently on the ass. "Okay, you. I'll take my cell phone, but don't be surprised if you can't reach me—there's not very good reception where I'm going." He turned and gave Eli a polite nod, and then he dissolved into a silver mist that flowed toward the window, went out through it, and was gone.

Eli was neither surprised nor scandalized to learn the three of them were intimate. Werewolves who hadn't yet met their mate didn't live in celibacy, and playing with one or two other people—sometimes more—wasn't uncommon. Eli had enjoyed his share of threesomes over the years. But he still found it difficult to witness their affection when his wolf wanted Arden for itself.

He put the untouched bottle of water aside and stood up, towering over the two other men. "I reckon we've done all we can do for one day."

"I guess we have." Arden turned to Eli, smiling ruefully. "Are you hungry? I can take you to the dining room, or if you'd prefer to be alone, I can take you to your room and have something delivered. I know you've been through a lot, and I want to help make things as easy on you as I can."

"I ain't hungry right now," Eli said. His appetite hadn't been as hearty as normal over the past few days, and he hadn't been sleeping well either. He wasn't sure he'd be able to sleep well again until he'd found his pack mates. "I'd rather go to my room."

"All right." Arden looked at Whimsy. "Can you come and make sure there are enough protections for Eli? We don't want to take a chance of the other pack tracking him down."

"Sure, no problem." Whimsy gave Eli a friendly smile. "The security on this place is already pretty good, but I can add some specialized wards."

They left Arden's office and went past the desk again, to a corridor that led to a back verandah. There were people sitting around at tables eating dinner, but Arden moved toward a set of stairs leading down to a path paved with natural stones.

"I'm giving you one of the cabins by the water," Arden explained, looking up at Eli. "It's peaceful and quiet, and the cabins are set apart from one another. It means you can come and go as you please and even transform if you'd like to. You'll be able to scent the magical boundaries easily enough. Just stay inside them, and you won't freak out any of the humans."

The thought of losing himself in the now of wolf form was appealing, and Eli was grateful for the freedom to transform even though he was far from the woods of home.

"I appreciate it," he said.

"No problem. I just wish I could do more," Arden replied, his voice husky. He stopped in front of a cozy-looking log cabin and opened the door. "Here you go. I'll key the lock to you inside."

Both inside and out, the cabin reminded Eli of the simple houses his pack had lived in, and he felt right at home.

"I like it," he said, giving Arden a slight smile.

Arden beamed at him as though he'd hung the moon. "I'm glad. Here, press your hand to the back of the door, and it'll make it open only for you. The wee folk have their own means of entry, and they won't come if you're around anyway. Just don't drink their bowl of milk on the hearth."

"I know better than to do that," Eli said as he pressed his hand to the door as instructed. He felt a tingle of magic as the door attuned itself to him.

Whimsy circled the room with both hands raised, his fingers dancing as he formed mystic symbols. "The wards are good," he said. "I added a couple of layers, though. If another werewolf approaches, it'll keep them out unless you let them pass."

"Good work, Whimsy." Arden turned his smile on his

friend. "Okay, Eli, you're good. If you want anything to eat, just pick up the handset and press nine. If you need to reach me, I'm 321—that number will even reach me on my cell if I'm off the property."

"Thanks. I appreciate all you're doing to help me." Eli wasn't sure how he could repay Arden for helping with the investigation, but at least he could repay him for the hospitality. "I'll pay just like any other guest."

"We'll discuss that at another time," Arden said, waving a hand. "Right now, you just concentrate on you and what you need, and what I—or any of us—can do to help you. You're part of the Asheville family now, you know, and we take care of our own."

The mention of family made Eli's heart twist, but he nodded. "All right, then."

"Well, then, I hope you sleep well—or as well as you can," Arden said. "Call me for any reason. I really don't mind." With that, he beckoned to Whimsy and turned for the door.

Eli waited until they were gone, and then he transformed to explore the cabin and its grounds, familiarizing himself with its sights and scents. Afterward, he was tired, but he didn't want to try to sleep in human form. As soon as he closed his eyes, he saw his pack again. Instead, he curled up in the middle of the bed in wolf form. He could remain grounded in the now easier that way, and he needed the rest. It helped, too, that he didn't have to worry about remaining on guard; he was safe here, and it wasn't long before he drifted off to sleep.

CHAPTER 3

*M*ost nights, Arden slept like a baby. Once his head hit the pillow, he was out like a light. Unless, of course, someone was sharing his bed, which happened with less frequency over the last ten years or so. He still had an active social life, but he'd begun working longer hours after building his second resort, the Hilltop. When he felt the need for intimacy, he tended to gravitate toward Whimsy and Julian and one or two other longtime partners, rather than jumping in to find someone new and exciting.

But after having dinner with Whimsy, Arden had kissed his friend good night and gone to bed alone. He told himself it was because he'd had a busy day, and the next day promised to be even worse, but the fact was that he couldn't sleep for thinking about Eli Hammond.

The werewolf was gorgeous—there was no denying it. With a positively leonine mane of dark, sun-streaked blond hair and crystal-blue eyes, Eli was enough to make even someone as used to beauty as Arden sit up and take notice. He was also huge and buff, and Arden was desperately curious to see what Eli looked like naked, although his imagination insisted on supplying plenty of images to taunt him. But it was more than just his stunning looks that appealed to Arden, and more, even, than the tragedy of Eli's plight. There was something *special* about Eli, and Arden felt drawn to him like a moth to flame.

Arden had, of course, noticed Eli's aura at once, and it had nearly knocked him out of his seat. Not all supernaturals could see auras, but Arden, like his father, had been born with the gift. Other supernaturals—such as Julian—learned to do it after a great deal of study and meditation, but most couldn't see them at all. And what Arden saw was stunning.

Every creature had a unique aura, determined both by what they were and *who* they were. Vampires, like Julian, all had a misty, silvery aura with different shapes and tones based on their age and if they were a good, bad, or neutral type of person. Elves tended toward golden, and dryads, not surprisingly, were usually green. Werewolves had deep crimson auras, but while the core of Eli's had been red where Arden observed it close to his body, it quickly became a beautiful, multihued halo that was almost like looking at the sun. No one Arden had ever seen had looked so bright, and that was part of why he'd *known* he had to help Eli, no matter what the council or anyone else said about it.

But thoughts of Eli kept Arden awake most of the night. He felt himself pulled to the werewolf, as though there was an invisible connection between them. It was odd, but Arden found himself wanting to go check on Eli in the middle of the night, to make certain he was all right and didn't need anything. Which was probably stupid, considering that Eli was an alpha werewolf who could obviously take care of himself quite well. Eli would probably think there was something very wrong with Arden wanting to cuddle up to him, run his fingers through Eli's hair, and just be close to him.

He finally gave up trying to sleep and went to his office, immersing himself in paperwork until his watch beeped at him at his normal waking time. Taking himself off to the kitchen, he ordered up an enormous breakfast of bacon, sausage, ham, fried eggs, hash browns, grits, and toast. When the cook had prepared the tray, he picked it up and carried it out to Eli's cabin, balancing it carefully as he knocked on the door.

A few moments later, Eli opened the door. His long, wavy hair was a sleep-tousled mess falling around his broad shoulders, and he wore only a pair of jeans that rode low on his hips. His chest and feet were bare, giving Arden an unhindered look at the sculpted pecs and washboard abs that had been hidden beneath his clothes yesterday.

Eli blinked sleepily at Arden and rubbed his neatly trimmed beard, but when he saw the loaded tray, his eyes widened with surprise.

"I didn't order breakfast."

For a long moment Arden couldn't speak; it wasn't every day that he got to see a warm, sleepy, nearly naked hunk of buff hotness up close. In fact, he couldn't remember ever seeing *anyone* as gorgeous as Eli before in the whole of his three hundred and six years of life. His mouth went dry as a jolt of desire as strong as anything he'd ever felt surged through his body, and it took a massive amount of willpower to force his eyes upward to meet Eli's gaze.

"You didn't order dinner either," Arden said at last, then swallowed hard. "I've seen werewolves eat, and I know you need a lot of food to fuel your transformation, and not eating is going to end up costing you eventually." He knew he was babbling, but he couldn't seem to stop himself, so he held the tray out to Eli. "Here. I'm not taking you to see my father until you've eaten properly."

Eli's lips thinned, and his brows drew together, but he

didn't argue. He *couldn't*, really, and Arden knew it. Instead, he took the tray, then moved aside so Arden could enter the cabin.

Surprised that Eli wasn't simply shutting the door in his face, Arden stepped inside and closed the door behind himself. "There's orange juice, and coffee and tea," he said, turning around and pressing his back against the wood. What he really wanted to do was to feed Eli by hand, but he didn't think that would be something Eli would tolerate. "And if you want more of anything, I'll go and get it for you."

"This is plenty." Eli carried the tray over to the table in the kitchenette, set it down, and took a seat.

"All right." Arden wanted to pace, but he made himself stay in place. If he moved, he'd probably end up over by Eli, and the temptation to run his hands over Eli's bare shoulders and comb his fingers through Eli's hair might be too much to resist.

Eli draped the cloth napkin over his lap and picked up the fork, and then he looked at Arden, one eyebrow raised. "You just going to stand over there and watch me eat?"

"It's a nice view," Arden replied, then could have kicked himself.

Eli turned his attention to his plate, looking down so his hair fell around his face, but not before Arden caught a glimpse of a flush rising in his cheeks.

"I don't like being gawked at."

"I'm not gawking," Arden said softly, feeling awkward, which was a very unaccustomed sensation. "If you want, I'll go and leave you alone. I didn't know what you wanted… it's not like you invited me to join you or anything."

"It's your place. I reckon you can do whatever you want." Eli pointed to an empty chair at the table. "Have a seat."

Arden moved to the table and sat down. "It's my resort, but this is *your* cabin. I was raised to not assume an invitation until I receive one." He glanced at Eli from beneath his lashes. "Besides, some people aren't too good in the morning, so I didn't want to overwhelm you."

Eli picked up a piece of bacon and nibbled it. "I ain't one to be grouchy in the morning."

"I'll remember that." Arden smiled slightly, wondering how Eli would feel about being kissed awake. Of course the image of doing *that* started leading him down a very dangerous path, so he folded his hands on the tabletop and took a deep breath. "I'm a morning person myself. It drives Whims and Julian crazy."

"You're with them?" Eli asked, that little frown line appearing between his eyebrows again.

Arden tilted his head, not certain why Eli would care. "With them? You mean, like in a relationship? Not anything formal or permanent. We're... friends. Good friends. We trust one another, and we respect one another's boundaries. I love them both, but I'm not in love with either of them—nor are they in love with me."

The little frown smoothed out, and Eli nodded. "Friends with benefits. We have those in the pack."

Arden knew it had to be hard for Eli to be without the companionship he was used to, especially as an alpha. He felt drawn to offer comfort, so he nodded and rose from his chair, moving to stand beside Eli and placing a hand on his shoulder. "We'll get this fixed. We'll rescue them, and you will have your family again."

Eli sucked in a breath at the touch, but he didn't flinch away. "That's my plan."

A tingle seemed to flow from Eli to Arden where Arden's hand was pressed against Eli's bare skin, and he wondered what it meant, especially since he'd felt the same sensation when they'd shaken hands the previous day. Unable to resist the temptation, Arden gently stroked Eli's shoulder. "I'm sure you miss them, and you're worried too. I know I would be if it was my friends and family who were in danger."

Surprisingly, Eli seemed to relax beneath Arden's stroking hand, as if the touch soothed him. "Yeah."

"I'm going to help you get everything you want," Arden said, continuing to caress Eli, hoping that support and simple contact really might be helping him. "I swear it. No matter what it takes."

Eli picked up the fork and began eating again, this time with more interest than before. "You're doing enough. Between your pa and the dryads, we should find out something to move forward with."

Arden was absurdly pleased when Eli started to eat, and he didn't move away, since Eli didn't seem to mind him being close. "It should give us a place to start, yes. We can play it by ear, see what clues we can discover and where they lead us. There's always a trail, and we'll follow it right to them."

"Damned right," Eli said, that low, deep growl rumbling in his chest again.

The growl Eli gave was one of the sexiest sounds Arden had ever heard, and something about it made him want to bare his throat and beg Eli to bite him. He shivered slightly, wondering if there was a chance that Eli might ever consider Arden as a lover. If things hadn't been so complicated, Arden would have made a bold play to get himself into Eli's bed immediately, but he didn't want to push when Eli was still preoccupied with the deaths of some of his pack and the unknown fate of the rest. Somehow, he didn't want to just be part of Eli doing some life affirming that he might regret later. No, Arden wanted a chance to have Eli for more than just a night or two.

When Eli had finished what he wanted of the tray—about half of what Arden had brought, which Arden guessed was probably more than he'd eaten in a while—Arden reluctantly stepped back. "While you get dressed, I'll pull my SUV to the front. Want to meet me out there when you're done?"

"Sure." Eli pushed back his chair and stood up. "I won't be long."

"Right." Arden took one last look at Eli's magnificent body, then turned and headed for the door, hoping he'd be allowed to see even more of Eli someday. Someday very, very soon, if he had anything to say about it.

It took Arden a few minutes to get his big SUV from where it was stored at the back of the resort and pull it around to the front, but not only did they need it for taking Whimsy along, he thought Eli might be more comfortable in the larger vehicle. He pulled up in front of the lobby and settled in to wait for Eli.

Before long, he caught sight of Eli in the rearview mirror, sauntering up the path from the cabin. He was dressed in the same red-plaid flannel shirt and well-worn hiking boots he'd worn the day before. He climbed into the cab of the SUV with far more ease than he had the Mercedes.

"Ready," he said.

Somehow, Eli managed to look just as sexy fully dressed as he did nearly naked. Arden cleared his throat to give himself a moment to find his voice. "We'll pick up Whimsy, then head to my father's place. It shouldn't take too long."

Getting to Whimsy's house, which was in an old, established neighborhood of supernaturals, took only a few minutes, and Arden pulled up in front of Whimsy's neat two-story house. The entire neighborhood was festively bedecked for the upcoming Halloween celebration, and Whimsy's house was no exception since he loved the holiday and always went all out on decorations. Arden honked the horn to let Whimsy know they'd arrived.

Whimsy emerged from the house and waved at them. He wore his hair in a long braid, and he was dressed in jeans and a loose purple tunic embroidered with alchemical symbols along the wide hem. He climbed in behind Arden and reached around the seat to give Arden a quick hug.

"Morning, Arden. Hey, Eli. How are you two today?"

"Doing okay, Whims. Thanks," Arden replied, smiling as Whimsy hugged him. "You know I'm beginning to get serious hair envy hanging around with the two of you. Maybe I should grow mine out long like yours. Maybe grow a beard too."

"You'd look good with long hair," Whimsy said as he sat back and buckled up. "A beard… I don't know. What do you think, Eli?"

Eli glanced at Arden. "No beard."

Arden chuckled. He didn't really want to grow a beard, but it was nice to have Eli express an opinion about his looks. "Yeah, I like your beard, Eli, but I'd have a terrible time growing one." After putting the car into gear, Arden set off in the direction of his father's house.

"I'll warn you up front about my parents," Arden told Eli, glancing at him quickly. "My father is very, very old, and he will speak his mind whether it's polite or not. I also think he's worked at divination for so long that he can't always tell when what he's seeing is the present or the future, so don't be surprised by anything he says. And my mother… well, you know about going to the elves for counsel, right? I've wondered if Tolkien was a supernatural or at least knew of them, because he hit that one right on the money."

"I can handle it," Eli said. "I'll do whatever it takes to get answers."

"All right. I just wanted to prepare you," Arden said, shaking his head slightly. He loved his parents, but his father could be disconcerting at times. His father disliked vampires, even Julian, because they were "unnatural." Arden suspected the real reason was because Gilorean had never figured out a way to do a direct divination on vampires, who were outside the cycle of life, and he didn't like to be reminded of his failure.

Arden asked Whimsy about his plans for Halloween, and the discussion lasted until Arden had left Asheville behind, turning along the westward route toward the mountains and the vast expanse of Cherokee National Forest.

"I'll get us close, but we'll have to walk a fair distance into the wild," Arden said as they passed the entrance to the park.

"Not a problem," Eli said. His features softened as he looked out the window. "It'll be good to be out in the woods again."

"I'm sure it will be."

A few minutes later, Arden pulled to a stop in a small clearing. "End of the line," he said, unfastening his seat belt and getting out. After Eli and Whimsy joined him, Arden led them to the southeast corner of the clearing. He made a complicated gesture, which caused the dense mass of thorny vegetation to part for him. "I grew up out here," he told Eli with a wry smile. "Next time you're tempted to think of me in modern, shiny surroundings, remember this."

With that, he led them into the forest that was still, in many ways, his home. Eli looked around with obvious interest as he followed Arden, with Whimsy—who was far more of a city boy than Arden—bringing up the rear.

"Do you like it out here?" Eli asked.

"Of course," Arden replied easily. There wasn't much of a path, but he didn't need one to remember the way home. "I know every tree, every dryad and naiad, and all the gnomes for miles around. When Asheville started growing, most of the forest dwellers moved further back from the city, and many of them ended up out here. The reservation where the Cherokee live is close by too, and the elves have a good relationship with the Natives. We have a mutual interest in protecting the forest and the animals."

"Is Tharn's pack the only one in the area?" Eli reached out and trailed his fingertips along the rough bark of the trees as he walked past them.

"There's a semiferal one deep in the forest," Arden replied. "They don't interact with humans. Tharn's pack is the only one close to civilization."

They continued on without speaking for a time, only the sounds of the woods around them. Then they entered a clearing, and Arden had the same sense of homecoming he always felt as he looked at the huge tree in the center, whose core enclosed his parents' home. "We're almost there. It's just up ahead. Home sweet home."

As they approached, Arden gave a piercing whistle, which caused the branches of the tree to rustle in obvious response. A door that was almost hidden in the trunk opened, and an elven woman stepped through it, smiling widely. She was as beautiful as most elves tended to be, tall and slender with shimmering golden hair falling to her waist, but to Arden she would always be just his mother.

"Amma," Arden greeted her, giving her a kiss on each cheek. "You remember Whims, of course, and this is Eli Hammond. Eli, this is my mother, Marin Goldenvoice of Calaena and Aquilan."

Eli made a formal bow. "Well met," he said.

Whimsy knew Arden's parents well enough that he could get away with kissing Marin's cheek. "It's good to see you again," he said.

Marin laughed softly as she accepted Whimsy's kiss. "And you, Whimsy," she said, then turned her attention to Eli. She grew more serious, stepping toward him and laying one delicate hand against his cheek. "I am so sorry for your loss," she said softly. "I know that no words will take your pain away, but the forest will sing for the members of your pack who have passed on. If you will honor us with their names, they will always be remembered."

Eli swallowed hard, but he didn't flinch away from the touch. "I'll give you their names," he said, his voice low and ragged. "They'll keep on living a right long time as long as an elf remembers them."

"I shall never forget, I promise," Marin replied. She stroked Eli's cheek gently, then stepped back. "Please, come inside. Needless to say, Gilorean has been expecting you."

Arden glanced at Eli in concern. He knew this visit was likely to be upsetting to Eli on many levels, although he hadn't expected it to start before they'd even stepped inside. But they would soon have answers, and that would undoubtedly help him feel better.

They followed Marin through the door, with Arden bringing up the rear. He smiled slightly. "Well, here's where I grew up, Eli. Maybe you won't think I'm such a citified elf after this."

Like the homes of many wizards—and elves—it was much bigger on the inside than it appeared from without. Still, it was homey rather than fancy, and Arden loved it. Marin was of a family that had a particularly close affinity for the trees. His mother had sung to the dryads, and the trees had shaped themselves to form their cozy nest.

Just inside the door was a single room, with large round windows that let in the green-tinted sunshine. Marin tended to spend her time on this upper level, and there were many tapestries lining the walls, since she was skilled at weaving. Near the back was a doorway to the bedrooms and a staircase of living wood that led downward to where his father spent his time among the crystals and herbs he used in his own craft.

"Go on down," Marin told them, returning to her loom. "When you come back up, I'll make tea."

"Thank you, Amma," Arden replied, then beckoned for Whimsy and Eli to follow.

He headed down the stairs, breathing in the scents of rosemary and lavender that he'd always associated with his father. At the bottom of the steps was another large room, and Gilorean turned from his contemplation of a large blue crystal in the middle of the space as they entered. He was very old, even for a human with a great deal of magic, with long white hair and a clean-shaven face that hid nothing of his years.

"Appa, I...."

"Yes, yes. Hello, Arden," Gilorean said, stepping past his son and going straight to Eli. "Ah. So you're the one. Big enough, aren't you? And strong too—I saw that. Arden needs a strong one to keep him in line. Don't let him give you too much sass, and you'll do fine."

Arden was struck dumb by his father's words. He was used to Gilorean spouting odd things, but this was even worse than usual. Eli appeared nonplussed as well.

"Not sure what you're talking about, sir," he muttered, although he wouldn't meet Gilorean's gaze.

"Tsk." Gilorean shook his head. "Too much unfinished business."

Arden finally managed to find his voice. "At the risk of telling you what you already know, Appa, this is Eli Hammond. He's come to you for help finding out why his pack was attacked."

"Unfinished business," Gilorean repeated. He raised one hand toward Eli and closed his eyes. "Darkness is coming again. They will walk among us unseen, and the voices of lost souls will cry out in the wind." He opened his eyes again and looked at Eli. "You were the first. You may not be the last, though the stream of the future is muddied and contains many eddies. They seek to increase their numbers, to expand until they cannot be stopped."

"Who are they?" Eli asked, frowning in obvious confusion. "Is someone after werewolves?"

"They seek that which is lost and should remain so, and destroy those who stand to oppose them." Gilorean shook his head. "I see no more, but there is danger. Great danger. Your path is shadowed, Wolf Master, and the path of all who aid you. And the dead who will haunt you are not your own."

"Appa?" Arden felt a chill of fear, and he moved to stand next to his father. "What do you mean? What dead? Undead?"

Gilorean turned to gaze at Arden, and Arden saw fear in his father's eyes. Then he sagged suddenly, and Arden caught him quickly, suddenly more worried for his father than about what he'd said. "Eli! Please help me get him upstairs to his bed. He's overdone it."

Eli didn't hesitate to pick up the elderly wizard and cradled Gilorean in his arms. "Lead the way," he said.

Arden turned for the stairs and went up them quickly. "Amma! Appa had a spell!"

Marin rose and went to the doorway at the rear of the room, motioning to Eli. "Through here. Just put him on the big bed. I'll take care of him."

Eli carried Gilorean into the bedroom and lowered him onto the bed, handling him with gentle care. "Will he be okay?" he asked, his eyes filled with concern.

"He'll be fine," Marin said as she sat down on the edge of bed. "You boys, go on out to the big room, and I'll get him settled. Arden, make the tea." She looked at Eli, her smile gentle and reassuring. "He often does this when a vision is very strong. Don't worry—he'll sleep for a few hours, then be fine."

Arden bit his lip. His mother had been saying the same

thing for the last decade, but Arden wasn't sure it was quite as harmless as she'd indicated. But he nodded. "All right. Whims can boil the water. Right, Whims? Faster than dealing with magical fire." He motioned the others from the room, then gave his mother one more worried glance before following.

"Sure, I'll take care of the tea," Whimsy said, giving Arden's arm a supportive squeeze before heading to the kitchen.

Eli remained silent as he followed Arden, appearing deep in thought.

Arden couldn't suppress a sense of unease—not just about his father's collapse, but about the dire words Gilorean had spoken. "I have a bad feeling about this. All of this."

Eli regarded Arden with a questioning look as he took a seat. "What do you think he meant? It don't make no sense to me."

"My father once told me that divination was the trickiest of the branches of magic for that very reason—it's as much about how you interpret what is said as what the diviner sees. Unless a path is very clear, my father sees *all* the paths leading from a point in time and must sort them out into something that makes sense." Arden couldn't stop himself from pacing restlessly. "Since you asked, I'll tell you that what I think is that bad things are going to happen. The kidnapping of your pack seems to have been the beginning of it, at least for us. But it doesn't tell us exactly why they did it, or what happens next."

Eli frowned, that little furrow appearing between his eyebrows. "It don't help to know bad things are going to happen if we don't know where or when or who's next."

"Doesn't it?" Arden shrugged. "You thought that the attack of your pack was just an isolated incident, right? Well, it's not. And we know we need to be careful, and that what we're dealing with isn't just some werewolf pack gone crazy. Dad said 'they' are looking for something that was lost and apparently will kill or take whoever gets in their way. So that tells us we really need to go back to your woods and look around for clues."

Eli rested his elbows on his knees and let his hands dangle between his legs as he mulled over what Arden had said. "Makes me wonder if the other pack was following someone else's orders."

"Possibly." Arden moved to stand in front of Eli. "Would a pack follow someone's orders if they killed the alpha? Or maybe they took half the pack hostage and threatened to kill them if the others didn't do what they were ordered to do. You still need answers, and we'll get them, but the answers might lead to even more questions."

"I'm guessing that'll be what happens," Eli said, scowling as he clenched his fists. His entire body looked tense with frustration.

Arden reached out, putting a hand on Eli's shoulder. "You're doing everything you can for your pack. Soon we'll have your answers."

"Good," Eli said, his features hardening. "I want to go home and start hunting as soon as we can."

"All right." Arden gave Eli's shoulder a squeeze. "And if Julian doesn't return by tonight, we'll go on without him."

There was obviously more going on than they knew, and Julian's "bad feeling" had apparently been correct after all. But Arden felt an urgency he couldn't explain to get started. He didn't like feeling like a sword was dangling over his head, yet he had the feeling that as bad as things were, they were going to get a whole lot worse before they got better.

CHAPTER 4

Marin hadn't wanted to leave Gilorean until she was certain he was recovered from his collapse. It was late afternoon before the elderly wizard was feeling well enough for Marin to risk leaving him alone, and then she'd insisted on feeding them all dinner first. As a result, the sun was below the horizon before they'd finally set out.

Eli could feel the mystical energy in the clearing Marin had led them to for the ceremony, despite werewolves not being as sensitive to magic as other supernaturals, which meant it had to be quite strong. The trees were tall with thick trunks, signaling their age, and Eli breathed deeply of the forest air, feeling more at home here than he had anywhere else, even Arden's resort.

The clearing was an almost perfect circle, and the trees opened up to reveal the night sky overhead. The moon provided sufficient light for everyone but Whimsy, who didn't have the enhanced night vision of werewolves or elves, but he'd conjured a small glowing ball to provide enough light that he could see the path that wound through the woods without tripping over any stray roots.

Marin stood in the center of the clearing and beckoned to Eli, who joined her. "Are you ready?"

"Yes, ma'am," Eli said. "What do we do?"

"Speak their names one at a time."

Eli's heart constricted, and he had to swallow hard before he could speak the first name. "Herschel," he said, thinking about the man who had been his mentor and friend. Herschel was the oldest werewolf Eli had ever known, and he'd led the pack for several decades. He'd had long white hair and a thick beard, and they had all called him "Santa" to tease him. "Herschel White."

Arden had come up beside his mother, and as Marin's pure, sweet soprano rose on the night air, intoning an entreaty to the forest to listen and pay heed, Arden's smooth tenor joined in exquisite harmony. They sang Herschel's name in English, then in Elvish, before entreating the forest to remember him always, not for the tragedy of his death, but for his life as a beloved member of Eli's pack.

The feeling of magic in the air grew stronger, and Eli saw dryads stepping out from the trunks of their trees, listening as the elves sang. When the last note of the lament for Herschel faded away, Marin looked at Eli again, nodding slightly to signal him to speak the next name.

"Lori Granger," Eli said, his voice growing husky. "Dale Holloway…. Andrea Holden…. Sam Cooper…."

With each name he spoke, Eli's grief welled up, and tears stung his eyelids. Yet as the song continued, more and more of the forest denizens came out to listen. The natural creatures like deer and bears kept to the periphery, out of direct sight, but he caught their scent on the night breeze. The magical creatures weren't quite so shy; in addition to the dryads, he saw a small cluster of wee folk, and a coyote shifter came up to stand close to Whimsy, head bowed in respect. There were other elves, an elderly couple with pure white hair, who added their voices to the chorus as the entire forest seemed to mourn for Eli's loss.

After speaking the last name, Eli transformed, threw back his head, and howled, adding his voice to the song. Hearing the song of mourning and remembrance lanced the wound on his heart and let his grief flow freely now that he had others to share his pain with. They weren't his pack, but they were here, and that was enough.

Silence fell in the wake of the song, and Arden knelt down next to him and buried his fingers in Eli's ruff, stroking his fur. Whimsy knelt too, and Marin flowed down gracefully in front of him, laying a hand atop his head, gently caressing his ears. Whining softly, Eli closed his eyes and leaned into the gentle touches. As part of a pack, Eli was accustomed to—and needed—the comfort of others; seeking out pack mates during times of loss, pain, or grief was normal, and Eli felt the lack of that support keenly. But more than that, his mate was touching him, and the wolf eagerly sought more.

"The forest won't forget those you lost, and neither will we," Arden said, leaning closer to him. "You aren't alone, Eli."

He shifted back into human form and looked at Arden. "Thanks."

"I wish I could do more," Arden replied, his green eyes searching Eli's face. "Do you feel like going back to the resort now? Or would you prefer to stay in the woods for a while?"

Eli almost said he wanted to stay, but he realized he didn't need to. The song was over, those who lived in these woods had slipped away, and Eli felt more at peace. For him, this place had served its purpose, and so he rose to his feet.

"I'm ready to go," he said.

The others rose as well, and Arden stayed close by his

side as they made their way back toward Marin's home. Several of the dryads nodded respectfully to him as he passed beneath the branches of their trees, and Arden spoke their names to him, apparently well acquainted with all of them.

After they made it back to the cabin, Arden and Marin slipped away to check on Gilorean. They returned within only a few minutes, and Arden didn't radiate the anxiety he'd shown earlier.

"He's doing a lot better," Arden reported. "We can go back to the resort to see if Julian's returned."

"I'm glad to hear it," Eli said. He turned to Marin and offered a respectful bow. "Thank you. It eases my mind to know the elves will remember our dead."

Marin smiled at him, raising a hand to touch his cheek. "They were a part of you, and therefore deserving of remembrance. I am glad if I could help offer some solace. It pains me to see the mate of my son so lost in grief and uncertainty."

Oh shit. Eli glanced sidelong at Arden, hoping he wasn't paying attention to the conversation. But Arden was staring at him, eyes wide.

"Amma… what are you saying?"

Marin turned to her son. "Eli is your mate. Don't tell me you haven't noticed his aura or felt the pull toward him. It is something elves and shape-shifters have in common—we both mate for life. I could see it between the two of you from the moment you arrived. Your father saw it as well."

Arden raised his eyes to Eli's, seeming subdued for once. "Did you know?"

Eli rubbed the back of his head and avoided looking directly at Arden. He'd counted himself lucky when Arden hadn't picked up on what Gilorean had said earlier, but the truth was out now, and he couldn't ignore it any longer.

"Yeah, I knew."

"Oh." Arden nodded slowly, then seemed to shake himself. "I suppose we should be on our way. Julian might be waiting for us."

Eli waited for a moment, but when Arden didn't say anything else about the mate issue, he released a quiet breath. Maybe Arden didn't want a mate any more than Eli did, so they could both ignore the whole thing and move on.

"I'm ready to go when you are," he said.

Whimsy looked back and forth between them, appearing confused, but he possessed enough tact not to say anything. "Yeah, I'm ready too."

"Give Appa my love," Arden said, kissing his mother on the cheek. Marin bid them goodbye, and Arden turned and headed out of the cabin, leading them back through the woods toward his SUV.

Eli followed along, feeling as if he was waiting for the other shoe to drop. Arden seemed subdued, so maybe Eli wasn't going to avoid a conversation about the mating issue after all. He hoped he was wrong; he hated trying to talk about emotional stuff.

Once they'd gotten into the SUV, Arden took out his cell phone, and as he turned the vehicle back toward the road, he dialed a number, holding the phone to his ear and steering with one hand. After a few moments he frowned, tossing the phone down on the console and glancing back at Whimsy. "Julian isn't answering. Do you want to give him a try? Maybe we should go by his house instead of the resort and see if he's there."

"If he's not answering for you, he won't answer for me," Whimsy pointed out. "Let's swing by the house first, although my guess is he's gotten obsessed with something and lost track of time."

"I just wish he'd told us where he was going." Arden bit his lip. "It would be just like him to go off and get into trouble on his own, and then expect us to come running to the rescue."

"Which we will, but I think he'll be okay," Whimsy said, although there was an undercurrent of concern in his voice. "If he's not at the house, I'll try scrying for him when we get back to the resort, okay?"

"I guess it will have to be—we don't have many other options," Arden replied, then fell silent.

When they reached the main road, instead of turning east in the direction of the resort, Arden headed toward the north. The forest gave way to rolling hills, and as they crested a rise, Eli could make out a huge house silhouetted against the sky. As they drew closer, he could see that it was like something out of a monster movie, all gothic spikes and spires and black ironwork. There were even gargoyles perched menacingly on the corners of the roof.

"There it is, Castle Schaden," Arden said. "Julian's sense of humor has always been bizarre."

"It's real atmospheric," Eli said, trying to be diplomatic.

Whimsy chuckled. "Wait until you see the inside. It's positively medieval. He won a bet with George Washington Vanderbilt, then used the money to bring this place from somewhere in Eastern Europe, stone by stone. He said that the Biltmore Estate was too pretty, so the area needed something to balance out all the gilt and crystal."

"It does that well enough," Eli said. "I reckon it's real popular at Halloween."

"Actually, Julian has the place warded to the rafters," Arden said quietly. "Normal humans can't come any closer than the gate without his permission. I think he stopped being amused by it all after Vanderbilt ended up dying so young, because it's a reminder that his friend was only human, and humans die."

"That they do," Eli said softly, thinking about the humans

he'd known over the years. He'd seen them grow old and die while he still appeared to be in his twenties even though he was a little over a hundred and fifty years old.

As they approached the massive iron gate in the stone wall that seemed to surround the house, Arden pushed a button on the visor, and the gate obediently swung open. The driveway was long and winding, with a single massive oak tree in the circle in front of the house.

"I don't think he's home," Arden said, looking up at the darkened windows. "But I guess we might as well check."

The front door was—predictably, almost—made up of massive wooden beams bound with iron. Arden produced an old-fashioned iron skeleton key from a pocket in his jacket and opened the door.

"Julian!" Arden called out, his voice echoing from the stones of the two-story foyer.

Eli stood in the middle of the foyer and tilted his head as he listened. Closing his eyes, he tried to pick up on footsteps or any other sound that would alert him to Julian's presence, but there was only silence.

"He ain't here," he said, opening his eyes and turning to Arden.

Arden nodded, looking troubled. He tried calling Julian's cell phone again, but it was obvious there wasn't any answer.

"I guess we'll head back to the resort to wait." Arden frowned in thought, then looked at Whimsy. "Unless scrying from here would be more effective?"

"Doing it here might help, given his energy is all over the place," Whimsy said. "He's got a crystal ball in the training room. I can use that."

"That makes sense," Arden said, then turned toward the back of the foyer.

There were several doors along the back wall, and he opened one on the right, which revealed a large, open room.

As they stepped inside, lights came up, showing a floor that had been padded with mats and a series of large illustrations along the walls, displaying various supernatural creatures, mostly demons and others of the soulless. There were also weapons in racks and a large shelving unit stuffed with books, scrolls, and small boxes. Perched on the highest shelf was a dusty-looking crystal orb, wedged in between two leather-bound tomes that looked older than Eli.

"Could you get that for me?" Whimsy gave Eli a beguiling look and pointed at the crystal ball.

The shelf was in easy reach for Eli, and he got the ball and handed it carefully to Whimsy, who beamed up at him.

"Thanks! Too bad wizards don't mate for life, or I'd be putting in a request for a tall, hunky werewolf of my own," Whimsy said as he carried the ball over to a well-lit area on the mat and sat down.

Eli glanced at Arden, uncertain of what to do since he'd never seen a wizard at work up close before. He finally sat down cross-legged on the mat and watched as Whimsy wiped off the ball with his sleeve, before passing one long-fingered hand over its surface.

Arden seemed to hesitate as well, then dropped down next to Whimsy, giving Eli a wide berth. "I hope you can see where he is."

"Me too."

Whimsy focused his attention on the crystal ball, and Eli watched with curious interest, wondering if he was going to rattle off magic words or go into a trance. But Whimsy did neither, and from Eli's perspective, the crystal ball didn't change, but based on his intense expression, Whimsy saw *something* in it.

"It's trying to home in, but it can't," Whimsy said, hunching over the ball close enough that his nose almost touched it, as if that would help clear the vision. "Fucker probably went into a warded area. That, or he's too far away to get a clear lock on him."

Arden scowled, the expression looking out of place on his normally pleasant face. "Damn it. Now what do we do? Just wait for him to come back? After what my father said, it's obvious that Julian was probably right about whatever he thought was going on, but we don't have a clue what it was."

"We don't have much of a choice but to wait," Whimsy said, looking worried. "We don't know where he went, and scrying didn't work, so we're pretty much out of options."

"Well, I guess we might as well go back to the resort." Arden turned his head and looked at Eli. For the first time, instead of smiling, or gazing at Eli in concern, Arden appeared guarded. "We can give him until morning, and then I guess we should head for where that other pack is. I'm not going to sit around waiting for Julian to grace us with his presence."

The wolf wasn't happy about Arden keeping his distance; after knowing its mate's touch once, it was greedy for more, and it whined at Eli, who hushed it sternly.

"Sounds like a plan," Eli said as he stood up. "Want me to put that back?"

"Yes, please." Whimsy handed the crystal ball to Eli before rising to his feet, and he offered his hand to Arden to help him up.

Arden took Whimsy's hand, rising with natural grace. "I'm tempted to steal his favorite bottle of bourbon," he groused. "I just hope he's not gotten in over his head."

"I do too, but there's nothing we can do about it even if he has," Whimsy said.

Eli replaced the crystal ball on the shelf, then rejoined Arden and Whimsy. "True enough. I'm in favor of leaving in the morning if he ain't back."

"All right." Arden sighed, then turned for the door.

After locking the front door, Arden drove them back to the resort. He pulled up in the front, got out of the SUV, and stopped at the base of the porch stairs to look at Eli. "I'll see you in the morning, I guess," he said. "If you need anything, I'll be in my office for a while."

Eli exited the vehicle, but he didn't follow Arden, even though the wolf was whining and clamoring to stay with its mate. It wanted the comfort of closeness and touch, wanted to curl itself around its mate and feel the connection they shared. But Eli didn't want the complications that would inevitably follow.

"I'll be fine," he said finally. "See you in the morning."

With that, he headed to his cabin without looking back, ignoring the wolf's mournful howls every step of the way.

CHAPTER 5

*A*rden went straight to his office, not even waiting to see if Whimsy followed. For once he ignored every greeting called out to him, moving so quickly and purposefully that members of his staff frowned in worry. Once he'd made it to the safety of his private sanctuary, he went directly to the liquor cabinet, picked up a bottle of bourbon, and poured a glass almost full. He tossed it back, shuddering in reaction as the strong alcohol burned a path down to his stomach.

Mate. Eli was his *mate.*

Of course Arden knew that elves mated for life—hadn't he seen it with his own parents? But he was still relatively young, even for a half-elf, and he supposed he'd never thought it would happen to him. What purpose was there for it, really? He was gay, so genetics never entered into the equation. When he'd thought about it, which was rarely, he'd wondered if by some quirk of fate he'd find out he was supposed to be with a female elf, which wouldn't have suited him at all, so he'd avoided the females of his own kind as much as possible.

Finding out his destiny was to be with a big, buff, gorgeous werewolf would probably have made him turn handsprings and dance around giddily under any other circumstances, but this situation wasn't even close to normal. Arden got the distinct impression that Eli didn't want a mate, and specifically didn't want *him*. Surely after everything he'd been through, shouldn't Eli have been happy to find his mate and realize he had someone to stand beside him and help him in his time of need? Wouldn't he have at least told Arden what was going on?

"Pour me one of those too, will you?"

Arden turned to see Whimsy walking into the office. Whimsy closed the door behind himself and leaned against it, watching Arden with concern in his eyes.

"It's definitely been one of those days," he said.

"You think?" Arden pulled another glass off the shelf and poured Whimsy a generous amount before handing him the glass, then took the time to refill his own. "I keep wondering if I've fallen asleep and gotten caught up in some weird dream." He rubbed his forehead. "What a mess."

Whimsy plopped down in a chair across from Arden's desk and took a sip. "I'm a lot more worried now than I was before we visited your parents, that's for sure. About what's going on with that pack, about Julian… about you."

"I'm really hoping Julian hasn't gotten himself into a situation he can't handle." Arden moved to perch on the corner of his desk, looking down at Whimsy and shaking his head. "We'll deal with the pack as soon as we can, because now I want answers too." He took another sip of bourbon, then stared at the amber liquid remaining in his glass. "A lot of answers."

"Some of them from Eli, I assume." Whimsy arched one eyebrow at him. "Or are we not going to talk about the elephant in the room?"

Arden grimaced. "We can talk about it, but I'm not exactly sure talking is going to make any difference. He knew, he didn't tell me, so he obviously doesn't want me. Not much arguing with that, is there?"

"I don't know why he didn't tell you, but he *does* want you," Whimsy said.

"What?" Arden laughed mirthlessly. "I've actually been interested in him since the moment I saw him, doing everything I can to help him because I thought I just wanted to help someone who really needed it. Trust me, he's not given me a single sign he's interested in anything more than what I can do to find his pack."

"He's been trying hard not to give you any signs," Whimsy said, inclining his head to acknowledge the point. "But there's a hungry wolf in his eyes when he looks at you. It wasn't your mother he was leaning against out there in the woods either. The wolf was responding to *you*."

He mulled over Whimsy's words for a moment, but they didn't really offer him much comfort. "I don't see how that changes anything, really. From what I understand of shape-shifters in general, they can control their animal selves quite well when they want to, unless there is some sort of magical interference like a curse or a sickness. Maybe the wolf wants me, but *he* doesn't."

"Sure he does," Whimsy said, giving Arden an exasperated look. "If he didn't, he wouldn't be trying so hard to avoid looking at you and touching you. I picked up on the vibes between you two, and I've been watching, especially him. I'm telling you, he's in denial, big-time."

"You really think so?" Arden bit his lip. He couldn't deny he was attracted to Eli and had been from the first moment he'd seen Eli in the council meeting. Eli's aura fascinated him, and he supposed he should have known from seeing it that there was something special about Eli, something that made him more important. "The thing is, I don't know what I should do. I'm not even sure what I *want* to do! I never thought I'd find a mate—a lot of half-elves don't. I've had a lot of lovers, but I've never been in love—never even come close. What if I fall in love with him, but he doesn't fall in love with me? How horrible would that be?"

"Why wouldn't he fall in love with you? You're smart, sexy, and a successful businessman." Whimsy gave Arden a shrewd look over the rim of his glass. "I think the real question is why would *you* fall in love with *him*? Sure, he's hot, but he's a redneck werewolf from Georgia who's probably never been out of his territory before now. Does he even have a job? I mean, what do you two have in common, other than maybe an affinity for nature?"

"How am I supposed to know?" Arden jumped up and began to pace. "He barely talks to me or looks at me, and it doesn't matter that I'm a successful businessman! Do you know he thought I was going to have some big modern hunk of glass for my resort? He figured that since I dressed well and had a sports car, I'm some sort of worthless ditherer."

"Oh, so he's a judgmental snob as well as an unemployed redneck." Whimsy tutted and shook his head. "Well, obviously he's not worth your time."

Arden glared at Whimsy, insulted on Eli's behalf, and then the absurdity of the whole situation hit him. He chuckled, relaxing a bit, finally recognizing what Whimsy was trying to do. "And Julian calls *me* a brat!" he said, shaking a finger at his friend. He looked down at his glass again. "He's better than that, I know. But that still doesn't mean things are all rainbows and puppies. If he's in denial, what can I do to get him over it? He didn't even seem to care that you and I and Julian have been lovers, so jealousy isn't going to help."

"You start by remembering who you are," Whimsy said firmly. "Arden Gilmarin gets the men he wants. Are you going to give up just because Eli poses a challenge? Maybe *that's* the problem! You've had it way too easy."

Was he going to give up? Arden wanted Eli, but that had been before he'd known they were mates. Did he want to be bound to only one person for the rest of his life?

Yes, you do. Arden had watched his parents for hundreds of years, had seen how they were always there for one another. Even though mages had longer life spans, his father was human, so he didn't have the whole mating thing going on that Marin did. Even so, it was obvious that Gilorean was the *right* man for her. Just as Eli was the right man for him, and *he* was the right man for Eli. Even if Eli didn't want to acknowledge it.

"Sex *is* easy," Arden replied. "It should be, or why bother? This is different, and that's the issue. There's more at stake than just a bedmate for a day or a year or a decade. This matters. If I screw this up, I'll never get another chance."

"Then take it slow," Whimsy said with a little shrug. "Woo him. Let him get to know you. Crawl under his skin until you're in so deep, he can't get you out again. You're his mate, and neither of you will have another, so you've got nothing but time."

"Time… and a murderous werewolf pack, and something bad looming over us," Arden added. "If I can get him to come out of denial, then I have to make sure he doesn't run off and get himself killed being a hero. He's got what, a foot in height and probably a good hundred pounds on me? I should be able to control him easily."

Whimsy laughed and raised his glass. "Take your clothes off! You'll be able to get him to do whatever you want then. Who needs strength and height when you've got a gorgeous ass just waiting to be pounded?"

"Well, there is that," Arden replied. He knew he was good-looking, and he'd never failed to attract any lover he wanted.

But Eli was different. He didn't want to screw things up, and he wasn't sure that sex would be the right lure to use. He'd have to think it over.

After tossing back the rest of his drink, he put the glass on his desk. "All my problems aren't going to go away quickly, but you know how to cheer me up, Whims. Want to stay over tonight? We can cuddle and plan what to do to Julian when he gets back."

Whimsy put his glass aside and stood up, smiling. "I'd love to," he said, moving closer so he could slide his arms around Arden.

Arden hugged Whimsy close. "I'm lucky to have you," he said, closing his eyes and letting himself be comforted by Whimsy's closeness. "You always know how to make me feel better."

Whimsy leaned against Arden and stroked his back from shoulder to hip. "That's what friends are for, right? I'll always be here for you in whatever way you need, even after you run off with your hunky werewolf mate and leave me alone with my cold and empty bed," he teased.

"Cold, maybe—Julian doesn't have much in the way of body heat," Arden replied, laying his head on Whimsy's shoulder. He stroked Whimsy's hair. "I'm not sure what he's going to think of all this."

"I suspect he'll be relieved." Whimsy continued rubbing Arden's back gently. "He's been pulling away again, and it feels different this time. I'm preparing myself for our play dates to be over."

"Really?" Arden raised his head so he could look into Whimsy's dark eyes. "I've thought he was just in one of his moods. But I don't want you to feel left alone."

"I don't feel alone," Whimsy said, giving him a reassuring squeeze. "Or at least I won't as long as you pry yourself out of your hunky werewolf's arms and hang out with me once in a while."

"Of course!" Arden promised. "You were my friend before we were playmates, after all. We'll have to hang out so you can tell me all about your new lovers and how hot they are. Assuming I end up with Eli and not crying on your shoulder, of course."

"You'll be with him," Whimsy said, sounding far more confident than Arden felt. "If you decide that's what you want, you'll make it happen. No one can hold out against you once you turn on the charm."

"I guess we'll see." Arden gave Whimsy a squeeze. "Come on. Let's go to bed. It's been a hell of a day."

Reassured by Whimsy's words and comforted by his presence, Arden led Whimsy to his private quarters. He might not know exactly what to do about Eli at the moment, but he'd figure it out. He had to, because if Eli was the mate he was destined for, Arden wanted to find out if they were as perfect for one another as the fates seemed to think.

CHAPTER 6

$\mathcal{E}$li wasn't long out of the shower when he heard a knock on the cabin door, and he frowned as he secured a towel around his waist. Fortunately, he didn't have to wear the same clothes when he got dressed. Tharn had driven over in his truck and left his suitcase on the porch while he was out the day before.

He hadn't ordered breakfast, so his early-morning visitor was likely Arden, although he was surprised. Arden had seemed rather subdued since finding out that he was Eli's mate, and he assumed Arden would keep his distance. But perhaps Arden was ready to get their road trip to Georgia underway. He knew Eli was an early riser.

Twisting his long hair up into a loose bun, Eli headed for the door. He considered getting dressed first, but he didn't want to leave Arden standing outside waiting on him that long. Besides, Arden was an adult and gay to boot. He'd seen half-naked men before.

He opened the door, unsurprised to see Arden was indeed his visitor, and Arden was carrying a loaded breakfast tray again. Eli stepped aside to give Arden room to enter the cabin.

"Morning," he said. "Come on in."

Arden's green eyes flew open wide, and he snapped his gaze back up to Eli's face from where it had wandered down Eli's body.

"Good morning," Arden said, sounding rather breathless. "I thought you might want someone to eat. I mean, something to eat." His cheeks grew pink at the slip.

Eli's eyebrows climbed, but he opted not to draw attention to the comment. Better to keep himself and Arden far away from the subject of mates… and mating.

"Thanks," he said, taking the tray from Arden. He headed back to the kitchenette and glanced over his shoulder. "You coming in or what?"

Arden stepped into the cabin and closed the door behind himself. "Julian never came back, but Whimsy and I are ready to go whenever you are."

"You sure you don't want to wait?" Eli set the tray on the table. "After what we heard yesterday, ain't no telling what he run up on."

"Which is exactly the reason we should go find that pack," Arden said, following along behind Eli. "If Julian was right that there's something bigger going on, we can't just sit around and wait. If he's in danger, that pack is the key to it."

Eli inclined his head to acknowledge the point. "Then I reckon we can head on out after breakfast. Let me put on some clothes before I eat. I'll be right back."

"You don't have to on my account," Arden said. This time he looked Eli up and down more confidently, and his smile was mischievous. "In fact, if you'd like, I'll take my clothes off so you don't feel self-conscious."

The wolf perked up with interest at that idea, but Eli

shook his head. "I don't feel self-conscious. I feel chilly," he said.

"Oh. Pity." Arden widened his eyes. "I can think of ways to warm you up."

Aw, hell. Eli didn't know what happened to change Arden's attitude from last night to this morning, but he didn't like it. He preferred Arden to keep his distance, not come up in here with wide puppy eyes and innuendo.

"I'll be right back," he muttered and retreated to the bedroom to get dressed.

He dawdled as long as he could, but there was only so much time he could take when doing nothing more than putting on jeans, a T-shirt, and a hoodie. He tried to visualize donning armor along with his clothes, and he returned to the kitchen, determined to ignore Arden's teasing.

He sat down at the table and looked at the tray, which was loaded down with too much food again. "Have you eaten?" he asked, glancing up at Arden.

"Actually, no." Arden inclined his head. "Mind if I join you?"

"There's more than enough here for both of us," Eli said, pushing a chair out with his foot for Arden.

"Thank you." Arden sat down, scooting the chair in before reaching for a slice of toast. "Whimsy was still asleep. He's not a morning person. But he is a good cuddler."

Eli clenched his jaw against a growl, reminding himself that he had no right to say anything about who Arden shared his bed with. Somehow the fork in his hand got bent, and he had to straighten it before he could eat.

"That ain't something I need to know," he said, a rumbling undercurrent in his voice despite his best efforts to keep it out. He liked Whimsy, but the wolf didn't like the thought of anyone else cuddling its mate.

"No? Does it bother you?" Arden asked. He took a bite of

his toast, nipping a section off neatly with his perfect white teeth. "I get that you don't want to be my mate, that you wish I'd just go away. That isn't going to happen. But would you at least tell me why? Why am I so unacceptable to you?"

Eli sighed, his appetite fading. He'd hoped to avoid this conversation, but he couldn't avoid answering direct questions.

"It ain't personal," he said, meeting Arden's gaze with reluctance. "I don't want a mate, period."

"Ever?" Arden put down the toast, obviously not having much of an appetite either. "You realize we only get one mate in our lives, right? That by pushing me away, you not only decide for yourself, you decide for us both."

Eli turned his gaze down to his plate, mulling over Arden's words. He'd been so adamant about not wanting a mate, he hadn't considered that he was making a decision for Arden as well. As alpha, he'd always tried to be fair and diplomatic, listening to what the pack wanted instead of behaving as a dictator, but he hadn't listened in this situation.

"Is this what you want?" he asked, looking at Arden at last. "To be bound to a stranger that ain't even your kind?"

"What I would like is a chance to get to know you," Arden said softly. "Mates are supposed to be the perfect match for one another, and I admit, I now understand why I was drawn to you from the moment I saw you. But we don't have to take it at face value, if you're not certain." He reached out, capturing one of Eli's hands. "But are you really ready to throw me out like unwanted trash, without even giving me— giving *us*—a chance?"

Arden's fingers were warm, and Eli's skin woke up where Arden touched it. The wolf whined, wanting nothing more than to draw its mate nearer—and Eli was starting to want it too, despite the complications.

"What kind of chance do you think this has to work?" Eli

frowned and shook his head. "Your roots are here. Assuming we get any of my pack mates out alive, they're gonna want to go home. So am I. Maybe you have more of an affinity for nature than I thought, but you ain't a werewolf, and you ain't used to living like we do."

"It has no chance at all to work if you aren't even willing to try." Arden sighed. "No, I'm not a werewolf, and you're not an elf, but that doesn't have to be an obstacle, unless you want it to be one."

"Maybe you don't think it's an obstacle, but there are plenty more to take its place." Eli pulled his hand free from Arden's grasp. "Besides, my responsibility is to my pack right now. I can't think about myself until they're safe."

A flash of hurt showed in Arden's eyes, but then he nodded as he schooled his features to stoicism. "All right. I understand that your pack has priority. And I'll help you rescue them, just like we planned. But after that, Eli Hammond, we are going to talk about this."

Eli didn't think talking would change anything. The problems involved in trying to mesh two completely different lives weren't going to disappear. But he didn't want to argue, so he shrugged and nodded. "Sure."

"Well, then." Arden drew in a deep breath. "Now that we've got that settled, I guess we should both eat, right? We have a long day ahead of us." He smiled slightly. "I suppose I should warn you, I'm a hoverer. I like taking care of people, if you hadn't noticed."

"I had an inkling." Eli looked down at his plate, but he didn't feel much like eating.

"If you aren't hungry, I'll have the kitchen pack some sandwiches for us to take with us," Arden said quietly. "I know you must be anxious to get going."

"Yeah, I am." Eli stood up, eager to move, to do something constructive to help his missing pack mates.

"Let's go." Arden pushed back his chair and rose, and when Eli stepped around the table, he reached out and put a hand on Eli's arm. "I will ask one thing. Please be careful, and don't rush in without thinking, no matter what we discover, all right? I can take care of myself in a fight, just so you know, but I don't think I'd be able to stop you if you lost it."

Eli sure as hell hoped Arden was tougher than he looked, because he looked like he'd break a delicate bone if someone gave him a little tap. How they could possibly be compatible in bed, Eli didn't know. If his mate were a werewolf, he wouldn't have to worry. Another werewolf—male or female—would be as strong and resilient as he was. Werewolves tended to enjoy vigorous, rough-and-tumble sex, but Eli figured that wouldn't be an option with Arden. Hell, he wasn't even sure what positions would work.

A fine choice you made, he grumbled to the wolf, who ignored him. Aloud, however, he said, "I'm an alpha. I got better control over the wolf's rage. I won't do nothing stupid."

"Good." Arden nodded as though Eli's word was enough to satisfy him.

Within thirty minutes, they had dragged Whimsy out of bed, Arden had gotten a cooler from the resort kitchen with enough food for lunch and dinner for all three of them, and they were in Arden's SUV, headed back to Georgia. Eli's truck wouldn't sit three comfortably, and they'd get there faster with Arden driving, so Eli was content to be the navigator for once.

The closer they got to his territory, the more restless Eli felt, and he sensed there was more than the call of home working on him. He wondered if he was picking up on whatever danger Gilorean had alluded to or if perhaps the spirits of his dead pack mates were waiting on him to mete out justice on their behalf before they could move on. Either way, this was not a happy homecoming.

He guided Arden to the secluded area where his pack had made its home for centuries. Their houses were spaced far enough apart to offer privacy while still remaining in easy walking distance. Some of the houses were almost as old as the pack itself, the remnants of log cabins built by the werewolves who had first formed the pack. Most of them were twentieth-century additions, however. No matter how old the house was, it was well insulated, sturdy, and clean.

They had to stop on the outskirts of the pack's territory; the road only went so far into the woods, and the main settlement was reachable only on foot. Eli got out of the SUV slowly, not eager to return to the place he'd once called home, the place that now held the worst memories of his long life.

Arden got out as well and came to stand beside Eli. Instead of his normal clothing, Arden had opted for a robe of elven design, in greens and browns that blended into the backdrop of the forest. It would have been easy for him to become almost invisible to normal human eyes, and he'd explained to Eli that since the dryads here didn't know him, he wanted to make sure they saw him as an elf and not a human.

"How far from here?" Arden asked, looking around at the trees, breathing deeply as though trying to learn the scent of a forest that was strange to him.

"Couple miles," Eli said, covertly eyeing Arden. He found it easier to see Arden's elvish ancestry when he looked like this, and he looked more at home here than Eli expected.

"But there's a path?" Whimsy asked hopefully. He looked like he'd never used the hiking gear he was outfitted in; there wasn't a single scuff on his boots, and his all-weather jacket was pristine.

"Yeah, there's a path," Eli said with an amused snort. "You'll be fine."

"He's not going to carry you, Whims," Arden said, giving his friend a playful smile. "Let's get going. I feel the forest calling to me."

"A guy can dream, can't he?" Whimsy said.

Eli remembered how Arden had made a point of mentioning how he'd cuddled with Whimsy last night, and he decided to get a little of his own back. "You get too tired, you let me know. I'll carry you. A little thing like you won't slow me down."

Sure enough, Arden turned to look at Eli, his green eyes narrowed slightly, making him look decidedly feline. "Shall we get on with it?" he asked, a slightly annoyed tone to his voice.

Eli gave Arden a placid smile before leading the way to the footpath. He didn't intend to put Whimsy in the middle of anything, but at least the interlude had given him a respite from the dread he felt over returning to his territory.

The path was well-worn and clear, and not even Whimsy had any trouble getting through. Once they arrived at the edge of the settlement, Eli looked around, trying not to remember how it had looked the last time he returned from a journey.

"There are houses in every direction," he said. "Stick to the paths and you'll end up at someone's front door."

Arden walked into the central clearing, and Eli saw him stop abruptly and give a shudder, as though he could sense the lingering miasma of the deaths that had occurred there. He bowed his head, standing silently for a few moments. Then Arden began to sing.

Apparently elves *did* remember, because Arden sang the names of all the members of the pack, both the dead Eli had buried and those who were missing but hopefully still alive.

It sounded different without Marin's fluting soprano, somehow more somber and sad. But all around them the forest sounds faded away, and Eli saw figures begin to emerge from the trees ringing the clearing.

Eli knew there were dryads in the woods, but he'd never seen them before. They were shy creatures who shared more of an affinity for elves and witches than werewolves. He hoped at least one of them had witnessed what happened to his pack despite their reticence about interacting.

By the time Arden finished the song, there were half a dozen dryads watching. They all looked sad and subdued, but one of them, who seemed older than the others, stepped forward, coming directly to Arden.

"We remember," she said softly, then glanced over at Eli. He could see that her large green eyes were shimmering with tears. "We saw, and we remember."

Arden raised his head, then glanced over his shoulder at Eli. "Are you ready?" he asked.

Eli hadn't come this far to shy away from hearing the truth now, and he nodded to Arden. "Yeah. I am."

Arden looked at him pensively, but then he nodded and beckoned Eli and Whimsy to come forward. "I am Arden Half-Elven, green sister," he told the dryad. "These are Eli of the Pack, and Whimsy Mageborn. Would you tell us of what you saw?"

The dryad nodded. "It was in the last light of day," she began. "Some of the pack were here beneath our shade, talking, when the dark pack came. They appeared as friends at first, but there was something wrong with their spirits, as though they were tainted. They asked the pack to join them in some task, but the old one, Herschel, grew angry and told the dark ones to leave. Then one of the dark ones attacked the old one, ripping his head from his body in a single blow. After that, there were more deaths, as the pack fought back, but they couldn't win. The dark ones were too strong and too many. They subdued the pack, then bound them and took them away."

Eli clenched his fists, rage washing over him, and he growled, a low and dangerous rumble in his chest. Every instinct told him to track down his enemies and kill every one of them he could find, but he forced himself to remain still. He wouldn't do his pack mates any good by rushing off without a plan or backup, and besides, he had promised Arden he wouldn't.

"Tainted how?" he asked. "Was it a sickness?"

The dryad didn't seem to mind his question, but she shook her head. "It was no sickness of the body. It was…." She paused, seeming to search for words for something she had seen but obviously not recognized. "Like a cloud over the sun of their spirits. A dark, malevolent cloud."

Arden frowned, then looked at Whimsy. "Something magical?" he asked. "Any ideas?"

Whimsy had gone pale, and he gazed at Arden and Eli with wide eyes. "Not any I want to think about," he said. "I hope it's some kind of collective mania, but the description of darkness and malevolence… that sounds like it could be demonic."

Arden's eyes flew open wide. "Couldn't it be a curse or something?" He seemed agitated. "Think, Whims… a dark mage? A druid gone bad? Please… anything but demons!"

"It's possible," Whimsy said, twisting his fingers anxiously. "We don't really know enough to be sure of anything. I'm not sure there's a wizard alive who could control an entire werewolf pack, though."

Eli didn't like the thought of demons being behind what happened either. He'd never encountered a demon himself, but there were stories handed down through the generations, and they'd always scared the hell out of him.

"If it is demons, what do we do?" he asked. "I don't know much about them."

"Not many people do," Arden replied. "The Demon Time was a very long time ago, before I was born. But...." He looked at Whimsy. "That's what Julian was worried about and why he wouldn't tell us. He's been watching and waiting for something like this for years."

Eli raked his fingers through his hair, feeling out of his depth. He could handle a straightforward physical threat, but this was beyond his experience. "I reckon we need to find Julian, then. Maybe he'll know what to do."

Arden turned to the dryad and bowed his head respectfully. "Thank you, green sister, for sharing your memories with us."

The dryad nodded. "Go in light, Arden Half-Elven, Eli of the Pack, and Whimsy Mageborn. I hope the taint of darkness does not stain your spirits as it did those others."

With that, she turned back toward her tree, and within moments the three of them were the only ones left in the silent clearing. Eli's protective instincts urged him to gather Arden close and take him far away from this place, never to return. As much as he wanted to avenge his pack, he didn't want to put Arden or Whimsy in danger in the process, especially not if demons were involved.

"What now?" he asked. "Should we go back to Asheville and see if Julian's turned up?"

"No." Arden shook his head. "I think I should go to where that other pack lives. We need to know. The dryads there can tell us what caused that pack to change, and maybe I'll be able to see where they're holding your pack."

"You mean *we* should go," Eli said, frowning at Arden. "The pack might still be there."

"And if they are, they'll scent you in a heartbeat," Arden pointed out. "I just need to get close enough to find a tree that can see. I don't even have to be on the ground—I'm small enough to go from branch to branch up high."

"You know werewolves can climb, right?" Eli said, resisting the temptation to grab Arden and toss him in the SUV. "They'll smell you too, and ain't no itty-bitty elf gonna stand a chance against a whole pack of werewolves on the hunt."

"They can't climb as high as I can, because they'll all be bigger than me, right?" Arden seemed determined. "Whims, do you have a spell to mask my scent in your bag of tricks? If not, I can do it the old-fashioned way."

"I can handle it," Whimsy said. "Just tell me what you want to smell like."

Eli drew himself up to his full height and stared at Arden in the way that made his pack mates whine and bare their throats. "No. You ain't going alone."

Arden raised a brow, seeming completely unfazed. "Do you think you can sneak in? I'm an elf, and you yourself keep telling me how small I am. This is what I'm good at."

Eli's pack mates never would have argued with him once he went into alpha mode, which underscored the differences between himself and Arden acutely.

"I don't care," he said. "You go with us or you don't go. Period."

"And just what are you going to do if they see you?" Arden snapped, narrowing his eyes as he glared up at Eli. "I can get in and out without them knowing. If you're spotted, you'd have to fight, and then what? Who helps your pack if you're dead?"

"I said no. It's too dangerous." Eli pushed down all the instincts that took Arden's defiance as a challenge to his authority. If Arden were a werewolf, they would already be in a fight, and he growled a warning. "It ain't up for discussion."

"Hey, leader of the pack," Whimsy said as he stepped between Eli and Arden and fixed Eli with a sardonic look. "You need to break the feedback loop, because if you lay a hand on Arden, I'll hex your ass so hard, you'll have spell damage for the next two hundred years."

Eli froze as the implications of Whimsy's words sank in, and he took a couple of steps back. "Aw, hell, I didn't even think about that." He drew in several deep cleansing breaths, and the coiled tension in his body slowly relaxed as the wolf receded. "It's the bond," he said, giving Arden an apologetic look. "If we feel something real strong, good or bad, it's gonna spill over."

Arden looked at Eli, then raised a hand to rub his forehead, seeming a bit shaken. "So it seems. I'll try to remember that." He glanced over at Whimsy. "Thanks for defending me, Whims. And for keeping a cooler head than either of us did."

Whimsy moved to stand beside Arden and slid his arm around Arden's waist. "No problem," he said, giving Arden a little squeeze. "Now let's see if we can figure this mess out. Arden, aside from the bond spillover, why do you think Eli's attitude upset you so much?"

"Because he's being autocratic," Arden replied slowly. He looked at Eli. "Thinking with his muscles, not his head."

Eli didn't like that description, and he opened his mouth to argue, but Whimsy stopped him with a warning frown.

"You'll get your turn," Whimsy said, wagging his forefinger at Eli. "Okay, so it sounds like you think he's being too controlling. Anything else?"

Arden bit his lip. "I think he believes I'm useless in the forest. And maybe he doesn't trust me to do what's right. Like I'm stupid and would attack a bunch of werewolves all on my own."

"Can I talk now?" Eli folded his arms and glared at Whimsy, who smiled placidly in return.

"Sure," Whimsy said, gesturing for Eli to continue. "How do you feel about what Arden said?"

"That it's all wrong!" Eli focused on Arden, wanting to explain before they could keep talking at cross-purposes. "Sure, I thought you were a city boy at first, but that was before I met your folks. I know you ain't useless in the woods, and I don't think you're stupid."

"Okay, good." Whimsy gave him an approving smile. "Then why are you trying to tell Arden what to do?"

Eli paused, gnawing his bottom lip. He could say it was because he was used to being in charge and his people doing what he told them to do, but that wasn't the real reason—and he suspected Whimsy knew it. He wasn't eager to tell them the real reason, though, because it would mean opening up to two people he didn't know well. Then again, Arden was his mate and deserved to know the truth.

"I don't want him going off by himself because I don't want nothing to happen to him," Eli said at last, turning his gaze to the ground. "I wasn't there when my pack needed me. I don't want to let no one else down like that."

Arden looked startled, and then his guarded expression relaxed slightly. "I didn't think of that. I'm sorry." He drew in a deep breath. "I didn't think you cared about anything but finding out about your pack. I was just trying to do that as quickly as possible."

The observation stung, but Eli supposed he deserved it. He'd been rather single-minded and pushed all other considerations aside, even his own mate.

"How about if Whimsy masks all our scents, and we go with you halfway?" Eli suggested, hoping a compromise would smooth things over. "I can probably hear you from there if something goes wrong, and I can get to you faster."

For a moment, Arden looked like he was going to argue,

but then he nodded. "All right. Are you good with that, Whims?"

Whimsy's answering smile was smug. "I'm good with it. You're welcome," he added with a pointed look.

Arden smiled slightly, then gave Whimsy a quick hug. "Thank you."

Eli squelched a little flare of jealousy and ignored the wolf's whining. He'd wanted to table all discussion of his and Arden's relationship, so he couldn't complain about Arden cuddling up to his lover now. Besides, Whimsy had shut down a potentially bad fight and gotten them to communicate better than they were managing to do on their own, and for that, he was grateful.

"Thanks," he said gruffly.

"No problem. I just want Arden to be happy," Whimsy said, fixing Eli with a hard stare that left no room for doubt that the threat of hexing was still in effect.

Arden kissed Whimsy on the cheek, then drew back and faced Eli. "All right, then, we have a plan. Are you ready to get started?"

"Let's do this," Eli said.

The sooner they were finished with this investigation and his pack was back with him safe and sound, the happier he would be.

fter Whimsy had masked all their scents with a spell, they set off in the direction Eli indicated led to the settlement where the other pack made their home. As they walked slowly, all of them scanning for danger, Arden couldn't help glancing from time to time at Eli and wondering if maybe, just maybe, Eli cared more about their bond than he wanted Arden to know.

It was probably just wishful thinking on his part, but Arden felt as though the pull between them was getting stronger the more time they spent together. Obviously Eli still wasn't pleased about discovering his mate wasn't a were-wolf, and Arden understood completely that Eli needed to focus on finding his pack, but at least Eli seemed to care if Arden got himself killed. Not that growls or bared teeth were the ways Arden was used to people indicating they were worried about him, but he was beginning to learn. He'd also forgotten that a mate bond could create a sort of feedback loop between them, and he was grateful that Whimsy had realized what was happening and put a stop to it.

Despite Eli's reassurances, Arden wasn't convinced that

Eli saw him as anything but a useless bit of decoration. Arden knew he couldn't fight a werewolf one-on-one, and he couldn't cast spells like Whimsy. Hell, he was even too short to reach stuff on a high shelf, but by the Most High, he could move in the woods without being seen! He wasn't sure if Eli was starting to care about him a bit or not, but one thing he knew for certain was that there wouldn't really be a chance for him and Eli to find out if they would really work out as mates until this issue with Eli's pack was resolved. Eli wasn't the only one who needed answers at this point.

Arden sensed the change to the woods before he actually saw or smelled anything. A sort of pall seemed to fall over everything, and he turned to look at the others.

"Do you feel that?"

Eli scowled as he looked around, and Arden got the impression that his ears would be pinned back and his hackles up if he were in wolf form. "I feel it. The air is tainted. It don't smell right."

Arden nodded. Trusting in his intuition, he touched a nearby tree, singing a soft phrase he knew oak dryads liked. It seemed to take a long time, but finally the green-haired dryad peeped out at him from behind the trunk of her tree, seeming wary.

"Green sister, there is a darkness on this forest, isn't there?" he asked her gently. She nodded warily, and he smiled to reassure her. "I'm looking for it so that I and my friends can remove it. Can you point me in the direction of its source?"

"South," she told him, pointing in the direction they'd been heading. "Not far. Too close, for it makes my roots shrivel."

"It does?" Arden didn't like the sound of that, but he didn't let his trepidation show. "Is it coming from where the werewolves live?"

"Close by there," she replied. "They are gone, but the shadow remains."

"Gone?" That was a surprise. "When?"

"Three suns ago." She shivered, and the leaves of the oak rustled. "They walked beneath my branches on two legs, and where they brushed against me, it felt cold. So cold."

Arden stroked the trunk of the tree soothingly. "I'm sorry for your distress. You're certain they're all gone, though?"

"Yes. There has been nothing moving in the forest. Even the birds and the other small creatures shun the area. We who cannot leave our trees are afraid it might worsen."

"I'll do everything I can," Arden promised. "Thank you, green sister."

The dryad faded back into her tree, and Arden frowned in concern as he looked at Eli. "I'm not sure what we're going to find at that settlement, but it might be even worse than we thought. Do you want me to go on alone from here?"

Eli studied Arden's face intently before responding. "No, but I'll trust your judgment."

Biting back the desire to ask Eli if he was sure, Arden nodded. "I'll be back soon." With a reassuring smile at Whimsy, Arden continued on.

He kept to the shadows of the trees, but he didn't feel the need to take to the branches. The air grew heavier the farther he went, and before long the feeling was so bad he had to force himself to move forward. Finally he came to a path, and as he peered ahead, he saw what was causing the dryad's distress.

Turning away at once, Arden hurried back toward Eli and Whimsy as fast as he could go.

When he made it back to the big oak, he was overwhelmed with relief at the sight of the others. Operating purely on instinct, Arden ran up to Eli, throwing his arms around Eli's waist and burying his face against Eli's chest. He needed warmth and reassurance to push away the horror of what he'd seen. Eli wrapped his arms around Arden's shoulders, offering a secure embrace.

"What happened?" Eli asked, his voice quiet and filled with concern. "Did you find them?"

"They're gone," Arden replied, shivering. Eli was big and strong, and Arden needed his comfort right now, no matter how complicated things between them were. "But they left something behind. Or some*one*. It's the most horrible thing I've ever seen."

He felt rather than heard Eli release a slow, deep breath. "You found a body?"

"Yes." Arden opened his eyes and looked up at Eli. "A half-transformed werewolf. They'd skewered him on stakes driven into the ground, and his blood had been used to draw a glyph beneath him."

"Shit." A growl rumbled in Eli's chest, vibrating against Arden, but Eli rubbed Arden's back soothingly. "Maybe we should all go back. Take some pictures of the glyph. I don't know jack about magic, but we got Whimsy."

"Julian might know something too," Whimsy said.

Arden didn't want to go back. He'd never seen anything so horrible in his life, and he never wanted to see anything like it again. He wasn't a weak person, and he could and did handle death; it was one of the things about being a long-lived supernatural in a world of humans, that he'd lost friends, acquaintances, and even lovers over the centuries. But he'd never encountered so much concentrated evil before, and he was finally beginning to understand why Julian was so paranoid about demons.

But if Eli wanted to go, Arden couldn't let him go alone. "You don't want to see it. You really don't," he said, burrowing closer to Eli. He was surprised Eli was willing to offer comfort, but Arden wasn't going to refuse it. "But I'll go back with you if you're going. I'm not letting you face that alone."

"I don't *want* to see it," Eli said, a pained look crossing his face. "But I need to know who it is, especially if it's one of my pack mates. We need to look for clues too."

Arden leaned back. Eli had no idea how horrible it was, but he was probably right—they needed to find out what meaning there might be to what had been left behind, and Eli needed to know if another of his pack had been murdered.

"All right," he said, then looked at Whimsy. "Do you want to go too?"

"No, but I will." Whimsy squared his shoulders, looking grimly resolute. "If there's any magical residue at all, maybe I can pick up on it," he said. He gave Arden a sympathetic look. "You don't have to go all the way back."

Arden glanced at Eli. He knew Eli thought he wasn't tough. Arden wasn't going to appear weak in front of Eli, no matter what it cost him. He pulled away from Eli reluctantly. "Thanks, Whims, but I can do it. It was just a horrible shock."

Eli released Arden but dropped one hand on his shoulder. "Seeing something like that ain't never easy. I reckon this was worse than most."

"Yeah, if it doesn't feel good all the way back here, I'm sure it's worse up ahead," Whimsy said, shivering and rubbing his arms.

"It is, but there's no help for it." Arden shivered, already missing the comfort of Eli's strong arms around him, although he appreciated the supportive weight of Eli's hand on his shoulder more than he liked to admit. "Come on—let's get this over with before it starts getting dark. I don't want to have to prove I'm a badass if the demons show back up after the sun goes down." He gestured for Eli to go on ahead. "I'm sure you know the way. We'll be right behind you." He put an arm around Whimsy's waist. "You can do this. I actually feel better about you going with us than staying back there by yourself."

"I feel better about that too," Whimsy said with a sheepish smile, and he kept one arm around Arden as they followed along behind Eli.

Eli obviously did know the way, and he strode through the woods, using his height and strength to clear the path for Arden and Whimsy. It didn't take long for them to reach the area where the feeling of wrongness grew much stronger, and Arden tightened his arm around Whimsy. "Do you feel that?" Arden asked softly.

Whimsy nodded, his dark eyes growing wide, and Eli gave a terse nod as well.

"It's strong enough even I can feel it," Eli said, glancing back at them. "I reckon it only gets worse?"

Arden laughed mirthlessly. "Oh yes. Much, much worse," he said. "Go on, let's get this over with."

Unfortunately, knowing how bad it was going to get didn't make it any easier the second time, but having Whimsy there beside him did. "Just a little farther," he said. "If you have to throw up, I understand—you probably feel it worse than Eli and I do."

Whimsy was already turning pale, and he tightened his arm around Arden. "Don't worry. I don't give a rat's ass about looking tough." Sweat broke out on his forehead, and he started fanning himself. "Dear Merlin... I've never felt anything like this."

It definitely seemed to be affecting Whimsy worse than him or Eli, and Arden tightened his arm. While he and Eli were reacting to the way the forest felt, no doubt the actual dark magic was what was taking a toll on Whimsy—black magic and white magic couldn't coexist in the same place. "Do you want to stop? If it gets to be too much, I won't be able to carry you."

For a moment, Whimsy looked like he might protest, but then he nodded and released Arden with reluctance. "I don't want to hold you back, and to be honest, I feel like I might pass out if it gets much worse. Take pictures of anything that looks like it might be magic-based, and I'll look at them later."

Arden hesitated, torn between following Eli to protect him and staying to protect Whimsy. He looked at Eli's back, then stopped. "Eli, I'm staying here with Whimsy. The bad energy is too much for him." It was a tough decision, but Arden couldn't leave Whimsy alone and defenseless.

Whimsy shook his head and gave Arden a little nudge toward Eli. "I'll be okay as long as I don't get any closer. You could go with him if you want to."

Arden looked at Eli. "Do you want me with you?" he asked simply.

"I might could use another pair of hands and eyes if you're up to it," Eli said. "You don't have to push yourself on my account, though." He walked back to Arden and Whimsy, waiting while Arden made up his mind.

For a moment Arden pondered the pros and cons, and then he nodded. "Could you lift Whims up into a tree?" he asked Eli. "I hate leaving him defenseless."

Whimsy marched over to Eli and held out his arms, looking like an imperious child demanding to be carried. Eli hoisted Whimsy up and placed him on a sturdy tree branch.

"All right?" he asked.

"I'll be fine." Whimsy leaned against the trunk of the tree and waved them away. "Go take a look at that site. The sooner you're done, the sooner we can get the hell out of here."

Eli nodded and turned to Arden. "Ready?"

"One moment." Arden leaned close to the tree, whispering to the dryad inside and asking her to watch over his friend. Then he straightened, giving Whimsy a reassuring smile. "All right. I'm ready."

Eli beckoned to Arden to move closer before setting off toward the other pack's settlement. Arden moved along just behind Eli, letting him take charge.

Several minutes later they reached the clearing, and Arden clenched his jaw as he faced the sight he'd been dreading. Part of him wanted to reach out and take Eli's hand or, better yet, burrow into Eli's embrace, but he held himself still, trying to convince himself it was no worse than watching a horror movie with Whims on Halloween.

Eli stopped at the edge of the clearing, and his features hardened when he saw the werewolf impaled on a tall stake.

"Aw, hell," he said, clenching his fists until his knuckles turned white. "That's George. Their alpha."

"I'm sorry." Arden swallowed hard. Horror movies were nothing like real life. They didn't have the awful heavy feeling of doom that hung over the scene before them. Horror movies didn't have the scent of death and something worse on the air. "I guess we should get pictures and then get out of here, like Whims said. Julian knows how to handle this stuff."

Eli prowled around the gruesome tableau, breathing in deeply as if scenting the air. "He don't smell right. That taint… I can smell it."

Arden didn't doubt that Eli could, though all he himself could smell was blood and death and the lingering sting of brimstone. He nodded, then took out his phone, turned on the camera, and began to snap pictures. He didn't dwell on the body, focusing instead on the blood-drawn glyph and the charred areas on the ground.

"I'm going to take a video of the whole scene," he said, switching the camera mode and panning around slowly. "I don't know what might be important to someone trained in this stuff, so this will at least get a bit of everything."

"Come over here." Eli beckoned him over and pointed to the ground. "Got some tracks. Looks like there might've been a scuffle."

"Yeah, it does." Arden was no expert, but the way the ground was gouged, "scuffle" was probably more like "desperate fight to the death." He glanced around and saw several houses set off from the clearing, just like Eli's pack had lived in. "We should probably search the houses, just in case… well. But if they were evil enough to sacrifice their alpha and leave him like this, they might have booby-trapped things."

Eli nodded his agreement. They made quick but careful checks of the outlying houses, and Arden was immensely relieved that there were no more dead bodies anywhere. Wherever the tainted pack had gone, they'd taken the rest of Eli's pack with them, presumably alive.

"We should look for the pack chronicle," Eli said, heading toward a house that was a little larger than the others nearby, moving slowly and watching where he stepped. "Might be something useful in it."

"What's that?" Arden had never heard of a pack chronicle, but then he'd never had much to do with werewolves beyond those of Tharn's pack who came into town from time to time.

"Most packs keep a chronicle—a written history of the pack," Eli explained. "Used to be passed along through stories. An oral tradition. But stuff got forgotten or changed in the retelling. Now most packs write it all down. It's usually the alpha's responsibility."

"Oh, that makes sense." Arden couldn't help casting furtive glances around, hoping the dryad was right about all the bad werewolves being gone. "You think it might have something we can use?"

"Won't know until we look at it." Eli examined the front door of the larger house before turning the knob.

Surprisingly, the door swung open, and Eli cautiously stepped inside, holding up one hand for Arden to stay back. After a moment, he beckoned to Arden.

"No one's home," he said as he entered the house.

"Well, watch out anyway," Arden said, glancing around cautiously. He didn't know if it was the whole bad atmosphere of the place or his intuition bugging him again, but he wanted to leave as soon as he could.

An antique rolltop desk was placed near the stone fireplace, and Eli went straight to it and rummaged among the drawers and cubbyholes. When he turned around again, he held up a leather-bound book, smiling triumphantly.

"Got it. Let's go."

"Yes, let's." Arden didn't need any other excuse for turning around and heading for the door. He opened it and stepped outside, skirting the body of the alpha as he headed for the path they'd followed in. "I hope Whimsy is all right. I'll never forgive myself if anything happened to him."

"He's fine," Eli said. "I can hear him singing."

"What?" Arden shook his head but increased in pace. "And to think I was worried about him. He must be feeling better."

"Maybe the dryad's helping him out, shielding him since he's touching the tree," Eli suggested, his long legs helping him catch up and keep up with Arden easily.

"Probably. I asked her to." Arden stopped when he caught sight of the tree. Sure enough Whimsy was seated on the branch, and the dryad was next to him, shyly combing her fingers through his hair while he sang to her. Arden rolled his eyes. "Do you want to stay here, Whims? We could come back for you tomorrow."

"No way!" Whimsy paused long enough to say goodbye to

the dryad before climbing down. "Did you find any potential leads?"

Eli held up the book. "Found the pack chronicle. That might help. Took a lot of pictures too. They killed the alpha, but he put up a hell of a fight before he went down."

Arden moved past Whimsy, going to the tree. "We'll come back and cleanse the glyph away," he told the dryad. "We need supplies to do it, but we'll make it stop."

The dryad smiled and nodded in relief, then slipped out of sight. Arden turned to the others. "We need to get back and find Julian. We don't have a demon hunter around anymore. He's the best we've got."

"I ain't heard tell of a demon hunter around here in a long time neither," Eli said. "Not that I know about anyway."

"They're rare," Arden said. "We used to have two, but they were killed in a car accident a few years ago. Shall we get going? Do we need to go back to your place to get anything, Eli?"

"I could get a few things from my house since it looks like I'm gonna be gone longer than I thought," Eli said.

"I want to get some stuff that belongs to your pack mates," Whimsy said. "I want to try scrying for them, and it'll help if I have something personal for the spell to lock on to."

"Sure, I can let you in their houses," Eli said. "How much do you need?"

"Maybe four or five personal items? Or more, if it's okay. Just in case... uh...." Whimsy trailed off, his expression turning somber.

"In case some of them are dead," Eli finished for Whimsy, his voice quiet and deep.

Arden could feel Eli's pain, and he put a hand on Eli's arm. "If they haven't killed them yet, I think they're okay, at least for now. Do you think you could track them? We know they passed by the oak dryad who told us they were gone, so maybe you could pick up a scent from there?"

"Worth a try." Eli fished a set of keys out of his pocket and handed them to Arden. "Key to every door in the settlement, including mine, which is the big one next to the common hall. Y'all get whatever you need for the scrying and pick me up some extra clothes." He paused, then added, "Please."

"You'll be careful, right?" Arden felt a surge of worry at the thought of Eli going off alone. "And you won't go too far without us?"

"If I get a good lead, I'll come back, and we'll all go together. Okay?" Eli gave Arden a searching look, as if seeking assurance.

Arden nodded. "All right." He gave Eli's arm a squeeze before removing his hand. "Hurry, okay?"

Eli shifted into his wolf form, seemingly as easily as breathing, and he shook himself once he was on four spindly legs. Werewolves were bigger than real wolves, and he could have easily rested his paws on Arden's shoulders if he'd stood up on his hind legs.

Arden couldn't resist taking a moment to look at Eli in admiration. Eli's fur was golden brown, like his hair, and he was big and sleek and graceful, every inch an alpha wolf. The wolf circled Arden, black nose crinkling as it sniffed the air around him. It licked the back of Arden's hand, leaving a wet patch on his skin. Then it lunged at Whimsy and used its weight to make him stumble before running off in the direction of the oak dryad's tree.

"Hmph!" Whimsy glared at the wolf's retreating form.

Shaking his head—even though Arden rather liked that Eli's wolf seemed to like him more than the human part did —Arden slid an arm around Whimsy's waist. "Come on. Let's get back to the settlement and collect what you think you need. I don't think he's going to find much, but maybe he'll figure out what direction they went."

"When we get to his house, let's just pack up all his dirty laundry," Whimsy said, looking disgruntled.

Arden smiled crookedly. "We'll all feel better when we get away from here. Whether I'll be able to sleep tonight is another matter."

They made it back to Eli's settlement, and Arden used the keys to unlock several of the houses. Whimsy gathered up an assortment of personal items from each building, and when he indicated he had enough, they moved on to the house Eli had indicated was his. Arden noticed that the interior was rather similar to the cabins at his resort, and he spent a few minutes looking at the neatly arranged furnishings. The cabin was obviously older and had a comfortable, lived-in look, with handmade furniture that included a huge sleigh bed with an antique quilt. There were bookcases lining many of the walls, filled with a variety of tomes both old and new, and on a little table by a big, comfortable chair in the parlor was an unfinished whittling project. Arden picked up the figure, which was a little wolf, and he admired the craftsmanship that had gone into the fine details.

He slipped the wolf into a pocket in his robe, then returned to the bedroom. Instead of a closet, Eli had a wardrobe. Arden opened it, selected a few shirts from the neatly arranged assortment on their hangers, then moved to a chest of drawers for jeans, socks, and undergarments and placed them on the bed.

"Whims, do you see a bag anywhere?" he called out.

"Top shelf in the wardrobe."

Instead of Whimsy's pleasant tenor, Arden heard Eli's deeper baritone, and he whirled to see Eli standing in the doorway, a hint of a smirk playing at the corners of his mouth.

"I'll get it. You probably can't reach," Eli said as he entered the room, which seemed much smaller with Eli's presence filling it.

"Size isn't everything," Arden replied with a sniff, though he was secretly relieved to see Eli back and safe. "Did you find anything?"

Eli retrieved a small suitcase from the top shelf on the wardrobe and handed it to Arden. "The scent went cold," he said, his expression turning somber again.

Even though Arden had half expected it, he was disappointed that he'd been right. "When we get back to Asheville, Whimsy can scry for your pack. I'm sure we'll be able to find them." As he spoke he packed the case with swift efficiency. "There. That should do you for a while."

"Thanks, I appreciate it." Eli closed up the wardrobe and then approached Arden. "Should I be keeping an eye on Whimsy? He ain't gonna fill my water pipes with frogs or nothing, is he?"

The way the wolf had teased Whimsy had been amusing, and had helped to divert all of them from the dreadful weight of evil that had been in the forest. In fact, now that Eli was back and they were away from the other settlement, Arden found himself a bit embarrassed by the way he'd clung to Eli after finding the body of the dead alpha. "You never know," he replied lightly. "Wizards, like elves, have long memories."

"He's protective of you. Can't fault him for that, I reckon." Eli cocked his head and studied Arden for a moment, and then he closed the distance between them and rested his hand on Arden's shoulder. "You okay? Seems like I could feel how scared you were. It wasn't real strong on my end, but it was there."

Arden was a bit surprised by the touch. Perhaps Eli really had felt his fear through their bond, just as they'd seemed to feed off one another's anger, and that was fueling Eli's concern. He had to admit, Eli's presence was comforting. He didn't want to read too much into it since Eli had made it clear where his priorities lay.

"I'm fine now, but I'll probably have nightmares about it for years." Arden smiled crookedly. "Thanks for comforting me. It really was a horrible shock."

"No need to thank me," Eli said, giving Arden's shoulder a little squeeze before releasing it. "What you saw ain't normal or right. Hell, it freaked *me* out, and I've seen plenty of fights."

"I don't think anything could prepare you for something like *that*." Knowing that Eli didn't think he was weak for needing comfort was a relief. "Is there anything else you need from here? Though I guess we'll be back in the next day or two, since we need to cleanse that glyph."

"Naw, I'm good." Eli picked up the suitcase and then nudged Arden toward the door with a hand at the small of his back. "Let's find Whimsy before he curses all my chairs to move before I sit down, and get outta here."

Arden gave a snort of amusement, but he moved to the door, eager for them to put as much distance between themselves and the glyph as possible. The sooner they were back in Asheville, the better he would feel. Of course they would have to return, once they'd figured out how to eliminate the evil, find Eli's pack, rescue them, and deal with the perpetrators, but not today.

CHAPTER 8

$\mathcal{E}$li slept later than usual the next morning, possibly due to the long road trip the day before, but he thought needing to recover from what he'd seen and felt was the more likely reason. Even though he, Arden, and Whimsy had varying levels of magical sensitivity, they'd come under mystical assault just from being in that tainted area, and he hoped Whimsy wasn't suffering too much in the aftermath since he was the most sensitive.

When Eli woke up, it was past the time Arden usually showed up with breakfast. Eli was a little more disappointed than he cared to admit that Arden hadn't visited. But he assumed Arden was sleeping in as well, and he understood why Arden might need extra rest after what they'd seen.

He ordered room service, keeping it light and simple since he still didn't have much of a desire for food. His appetite always suffered when he was worried about something, and his pack mates being kidnapped was the biggest thing he'd ever had to worry about in his life. After breakfast, he showered and dressed, and then he debated what to do next. He didn't want to contact Arden in case he was still resting.

He caught a familiar scent just before he heard scratching at the cabin door, and he went to open it, pleased to see Tharn outside the door.

"Morning," he said as he stepped outside to join Tharn on the narrow porch.

The big, shaggy gray wolf shook himself, and then Tharn shifted form. "Mornin'. Since you ain't bothered to call me, I figured I'd come see what you've found out about your pack."

"Not a whole lot." Eli rubbed his beard absently and tried not to think about the horrific things he'd seen. "Just enough to know this is probably bigger than we thought. We went out to the other settlement yesterday. Found the alpha dead. Not just murder, but a ritual death. There was a glyph drawn on the ground underneath him, and the whole place was tainted. Just about made Whimsy sick by the time we were halfway there."

Tharn frowned. "I don't like the sound of that. Been a long time since we had any problems with dark magic around here. There weren't no sign of your pack or the others?"

"Naw, they were gone," Eli said. "I tried tracking them, but the trail went cold."

"Damn." Tharn shook his head. "Sorry to hear it, boy, but you come to the right place for help. Arden knows folks, and Julian Schaden's got a lot of experience with the bad stuff. As much as it pains me to admit that werewolves can't do everything, sounds like you need that kind of help more than ever."

"Yeah, I think you're right," Eli said with a wry smile. "This is definitely more than a fight over territory."

"I had already sent a message to the closest pack to the south, to keep an eye out for trouble, just in case," Tharn said slowly. "If the bastards that hit yours are on the run, there's no telling where they'll end up. Might even try to hit someone else. I think I gotta spread the word around to the other packs I know that there's dark goings-on."

"You should," Eli said, nodding. "Gilorean said something about unfinished business and that my pack was the first, but not the last. Sounds to me like every pack in the area is in danger."

Tharn's eyes widened. "Shit. I don't know how accurate that magic of his is, but I ain't one to take chances, 'specially now. Gotta put a stop to this as quick as we can. I just hope we ain't too late."

Eli released a quiet sigh and raked his fingers through his hair. "Me too."

Tharn put a hand on Eli's shoulder, giving it a squeeze. "You got a lot weighing on you, I know, but like I said, you come to the right place, especially since you ended up finding your mate, because you could use his strength and comfort about now, I reckon. I was surprised when they told me you were out here. I figured you'd be sharing Arden's bed by now."

Eli felt his face growing hot, not just because of Tharn's bluntness but also because of the wolf's enthusiastic endorsement of the idea. "That ain't happening anytime soon."

"Well, why the hell not?" Tharn shook his head. "If you ask me, he's just about perfect for you. And you for him, for that matter." His expression turned sly. "Don't tell me you ain't tried to lure him away from that vampire he goes around with. Of course, Julian's quite a looker too."

Eli felt a flare of jealousy at the mention of Julian—who was quite attractive, he admitted grudgingly—but he was too surprised by Tharn's observation to dwell on it. "Perfect for me? How do you figure that? We ain't even the same kind of supernatural. He don't understand our ways, and I sure as hell don't understand his."

"Then you get the excitement of discovering things about each other. Did you ever think of that?" Tharn clapped Eli on the shoulder. "Boy, you are too serious by half, and I know it ain't all about the latest shit that you got heaped on your plate. Being steady and reliable is a good thing in an alpha, and at the risk of swelling your head, you are a damned fine one. Arden is just what you need in a mate—easygoing and knows how to have a good time, but he ain't flighty. And you're just what he needs—someone to ground him, someone he can lavish his affection on. He's a caretaker, that one. If you was to ask the supernaturals around here who is always the first to offer help, it'd be Arden. Did you know he helped found a home for orphan shifter children? He's got a heart as big as the forest."

Eli had noticed Arden's caretaker tendencies, but he'd chalked it up to the mate bond being at work. He supposed he should have known better, considering how solicitous Arden had been when Whimsy started feeling sick from the black magic in the woods.

"I don't know if I want someone hovering over me," he said, although there wasn't as much conviction in his voice as he would have liked. "Besides, he's just a little-bitty thing. I'd be scared I'd break him."

Tharn burst into laughter. "Boy, don't you know nothing 'bout elves? He's little, but I guarantee you, he's a lot tougher than he looks. Besides, I heard from some of the boys that he likes it rough, if you know what I mean."

"The boys can stop talking about him now." The words came out before Eli had a chance to stop them, no more than he could stop the surge of possessiveness he felt. He clenched his fists, annoyed with himself for rising to Tharn's bait.

Tharn grew serious and gave Eli's shoulder a gentle

squeeze. "Yeah, it's like that," he said quietly. "You can try denying it, but it ain't going away. Even if you're miles away from him, you're gonna be thinking about him, wondering if he's with someone. And others ain't gonna look so appealing to you now."

"Yeah, I can tell." Eli released a slow breath and uncurled his fists, forcing himself to relax. "I've put it on the back burner. Got enough to deal with already without that as well, especially since I ain't so sure this is what I want. The wolf won't let me forget, though."

"It's not gonna," Tharn replied. "You think you got a choice, boy? It don't work that way. What *you* want don't matter a lick to the wolf, now that it knows its mate. I suppose you could try fighting the wolf for the rest of your life, but it won't do you no good. The wolf is always gonna want to be with Arden. I've known a few who tried to resist the mate bond for one damn fool reason or another, and I know of only one that's been able to do it for long. And the one that did was the most miserable bastard I've ever known in my life."

Eli's stomach knotted up at that. He'd been giving some thought to suggesting to Arden that they part ways when this mess with his pack was over. He'd promised to discuss it, but he didn't see what good talking would do to resolve the differences between them. Now it sounded like that wasn't even an option.

"Miserable how?" he asked, hoping Tharn was exaggerating.

Tharn raised a brow, then peered at Eli closely. "As far as I know, he didn't have many happy moments from the day he turned his back on his mate. He was a proud one, thought he should be alpha of his pack but didn't have what it takes. Always lost out when it came to a fight and got real cocky, claiming he'd never take his mate until he won his rightful place. I felt real bad for his gal, too, who was as sweet and pretty a little thing as anyone could ask for. Drowned herself in a lake one day after he walked away and said he weren't never coming back."

"What happened to him?" Eli wasn't sure he wanted to know, but morbid curiosity won out.

"Ended up without mate or pack, living alone in a shack in the woods," Tharn said, then shrugged. "Brought it on himself, because no pack felt they could trust a man who rejected his mate out of pure foolish pride."

"Did that really happen, or did you just make up a parable to scare me?" Eli asked, raising a dubious eyebrow at Tharn.

Tharn's eyes narrowed, and he growled softly. "Why don't you just reject your mate and find out for yourself, you young whelp. If you're that damn stupid, you deserve whatever you get."

Eli held up both hands, palm out. He didn't want to alienate Tharn, and he wasn't keen on starting his day with a dominance battle either.

"I ain't rejected him," Eli said. "But I'm not gonna turn cartwheels at the thought of being bound to a stranger who's not even my kind neither. I got no idea how this is supposed to work out."

"Lots of mates start off as strangers, boy. I seen hundreds of mated pairs in my time, and weren't all of them werewolves with other werewolves," Tharn replied. "Mostly it was werewolves with other shifters, but sometimes werewolves with witches or wizards. Knew one male werewolf what found himself with a female elf, and you'd have thought he was king of the fuckin' world, as proud as he was for being so special as to get one of the Fae."

"What's so special about that?" Eli asked, puzzled by Tharn's comment.

"What, you don't thinks it's special to get a half-elf?"

Tharn snorted. "The way we see it in my pack, and most of the others I know of, it's a mark of an especially strong bond when a werewolf's mate's not another werewolf. Something about each of you completes something about the other and does it so well that things like your outsides don't matter. It means you're marked to do something special."

"We ain't gonna be making any babies that'll grow up and save the world," Eli said with a little snort. "Other than that, I don't see why we gotta be stuck together for life just to do one thing, whatever it is."

Tharn rolled his eyes. "Eli, I never thought you was stupid, but I'm beginning to have my doubts. Why are you so dead set against him? Because you ought to know if you reject him, you're probably gonna have Earl all up in your face. He ain't too happy that you waltzed in here and won Arden without having to lift a finger. He sure as hell wouldn't have no doubts if he'd found out Arden was meant to be his."

"Earl can go fuck himself," Eli snapped, unable to ignore the jealousy he felt at the thought of Tharn's second-in-command touching Arden. He drew in a deep breath and tried to push the wolf down, but it fought him harder than usual. "I got enough that's out of my control right now. I didn't need this on top of everything else."

Tharn held up a conciliatory hand. "All right, don't get your knickers all twisted up. I'm just saying, your mate can be a help and a comfort to you—something it looks to me like you sorely need about now. My Morag has helped keep me grounded in the tough times more than I should probably admit. I'm a better alpha for having her."

"I don't even know what to do with him," Eli said, a grumbling note in his voice as he folded his arms and scowled. "It'd be easier if he was a werewolf."

"Take him to bed. It'll all sort itself out," Tharn advised.

"You're thinking too much, son. It's not about your head, it's about your heart. More importantly, the *wolf's* heart. The magic's never wrong, and there's no sense in fighting it and causing yourself more frustration. And you're frustrating him as much as yourself."

"There's more to a relationship than sex," Eli said, still scowling. "My home is in Georgia. His is here. We ain't nothing alike. I don't see how this is gonna work."

"Morag thought the same thing about me." Tharn smiled slightly. "When we was first together, we fought like two wolverines with bad tempers. We met at a gathering, and she didn't want to leave her home in Texas to move to the mountains with a dirty, uncouth scoundrel like yours truly. But I was already alpha, so she didn't have a choice. She sure let me know what she thought, you better believe it, but it worked itself out. Take Arden to bed, and you'll see for yourself."

"How did it work itself out? She had to give up everything —home, family, friends. That don't seem fair. Sex alone can't be worth it," Eli said, giving Tharn a dubious look. He didn't like the idea of giving up his home, especially since it would mean uprooting his pack—assuming he was able to rescue them—but he didn't like the idea of taking Arden away from his resorts, his friends, or his family either, especially since Gilorean wasn't in good health.

"My family became her family, and it ain't like she couldn't see hers no more." Tharn shook his head. "Boy, it ain't just about sex, though that's like the icing on the cake. Everyone's life has losses. It's a fact you can't stop even if you wanted to. When Morag said she'd take me on, I vowed I'd love her all the harder to make up for the pain of what she was giving up. You ain't never known love the way two mates love each other. That's how it works itself out."

Eli thought over what Tharn had said, and while it made

sense—and the wolf was in full agreement—Eli still balked at the idea of opening his heart to Arden. Part of it was his stubborn streak kicking in. He didn't like feeling out of control of so many aspects of his life, and he didn't like major decisions being taken out of his hands. A larger part of it, however, was his belief that he and Arden weren't a good match.

"The problem with that is I don't love Arden," he said at last. "No more than he loves me."

"You do, you just don't know it yet, because you're looking at it from two feet instead of four." Tharn spoke with the certainty of total belief. "It's like this, son. You know a mother loves her child fiercely because it's *hers*—there's a bond there because she carried and birthed it. She don't know if her child will grow up to be a bad person or a good one, if he'll do great things or nothing at all. She don't know that child as a person, but she knows the bond, and she trusts it, and that's where the love comes from. You got a bond with Arden now, like it or not. It ain't of blood, but one of magic and biology—and don't give me no shit about you both being men, that's not what matters. You don't know Arden, true enough, any more than that mother knows who her child will turn out to be. But it don't matter, because the love is already there. You can't escape it. What would you do if Arden was to run out to you right now, hurt and scared and needing you? Would you say 'I don't know you, stay away,' or would you open your arms because he needs you and you need to be the one who takes care of him?"

Eli grimaced, unable to argue because he'd already answered Tharn's question with his actions yesterday. As little as he liked having the choice made for him, he had a mate, and no amount of fighting or wishing it otherwise would change that fact.

He only had two options. He could keep fighting the bond

out of sheer stubbornness, or he could accept it and try to make the best of it. Arden was his now, and Eli had never shirked his responsibilities. Besides, he couldn't deny the wolf's insistence that Arden was the one it wanted. Maybe if he paid more attention to his instincts than to the stubborn voice in his head, he could make things easier for himself.

He thought about how right and good it felt having Arden in his arms. He'd felt Arden's fear and *wanted* to comfort him. The thought of turning Arden away hadn't crossed his mind. The wolf yearned to feel Arden's warm, slender body pressed close again. It wanted to taste Arden's skin and breathe deep of Arden's scent, and Eli was having a much harder time coming up with reasons why he should deny himself those pleasures.

"I don't reckon you know anything about elvish courtships, do you?" he said at last.

"Me?" Tharn looked surprised, but then he laughed. "Damn, son, I ain't nothing but a backwoods werewolf. But I reckon what works for werewolves will work the same for a half-elf. Say nice things to him, give him gifts, then growl and pounce. Remember, if you want him, he's gonna feel it. Let the wolf guide you."

"The wolf wants to move faster than I do," Eli said with a little shrug. "The courtship's more for me than Arden."

"Well, then, do what you feel you want or need to do. Ain't no rules to this. But if you want to know what he likes, ask Whimsy Hickes. If he likes you, he'll help you."

Eli snorted. "Pretty sure he don't like me, but if he knows I'm trying to do right by Arden, maybe he'll help me anyway."

"Probably. And just remember, when in doubt, touch him —it'll help you both." Tharn smiled knowingly. "You'll figure it out, and in no time you'll be wondering why you thought it was so hard. And in the meantime, I'm gonna warn the packs. Let me know if you need me and the boys to help out with the hunt. You know you can count on us."

"Thanks, I appreciate it," Eli said, mustering a smile.

"Anytime."

With that, Tharn shifted back into his wolf form. He nodded to Eli, then ran off toward the woods. Eli watched him go and went back inside to trade the sweatshirt he'd put on earlier for one of his nicer flannel shirts. He trimmed his beard and brushed his hair into a loose ponytail. He had a courtship to plan, and the first step was making himself presentable.

Once he was satisfied with his appearance, he grabbed the keys to his truck and headed out to find a local nursery. They couldn't move ahead with the search for his pack until either Whimsy or Julian uncovered the meaning behind the glyph, and Julian wasn't even back yet, so Eli was stuck waiting, which he hated. But he could do something constructive about courting Arden, and he figured he couldn't go wrong with flowers.

CHAPTER 9

Arden stared down at the plans for the Riverside Halloween celebration without really seeing them. Despite the charm Whimsy had thrown so that Arden could sleep without nightmares of the sacrificed alpha, he'd still tossed and turned, unable to switch his mind off. He was worried about Julian, who still wasn't answering his phone and hadn't bothered to check in. Something could have gone wrong—it was even possible Julian had run afoul of the dark pack, but there was no way to know. There was also the matter of having to return to Georgia so they could cleanse the glyph, and of locating where Eli's pack had been taken to, if any of them were even still alive. And over and above everything else was Arden's growing awareness of Eli, and the effect they were having on one another.

Thoughts of Eli had occupied him most of the night, and he felt a bit guilty that with all the issues they were facing, he couldn't get Eli out of his mind. Maybe it was the bond that was affecting him, because what he wanted more than anything else was to have Eli's arms around him again. Eli had made him feel safe when he'd been as terrified as he'd ever been in his life, and he couldn't help wanting to feel that security again.

He completely understood that Eli needed to concentrate on finding his pack; they were his friends, his family, and they were in danger. If his parents or Julian or Whimsy had been kidnapped, Arden would be going out of his mind with worry, so he could imagine what Eli was feeling. It made sense that Eli wanted to put personal matters aside until his pack was safe, but logic had nothing to do with the way Arden was feeling, nor did it do anything to help him get rid of the feeling that Eli was going to do everything he could to resist their bond even after the danger was over. A part of Arden couldn't help feeling hurt at the thought of being rejected without Eli ever giving them a chance to see what it would be like between them. He'd only tried to help Eli, but it was pretty obvious that Eli didn't want him because he wasn't a werewolf.

Blowing out a breath of frustration, Arden pushed the paperwork away. He couldn't focus on throwing a celebration for the Asheville supernatural community when there was so much happening. If a dangerous werewolf pack was roaming the area, they should be doing something about it, but Arden had no doubt the council would be as ineffectual as usual about doing anything. They'd all lived in safety for so long that many of his fellow supernaturals couldn't remember times when there had been danger. Arden was old enough to have seen perfectly innocent witches burned at the stake, and he well remembered the way the Cherokee and other Natives had been persecuted. Even the ones who were as old as he was, or older, had grown used to their peaceful existence and didn't even want to consider the possibility that things could change. Julian had been the only one who'd felt that they were simply in the calm before a storm, and everyone had mocked him for his doomsaying.

Only, Julian had obviously been right to be concerned, and now Julian was off somewhere just when they needed him most, and possibly even in danger as well. The fact that Arden was bound to a mate who didn't want him seemed trivial in comparison.

Covering his eyes with his hands, Arden tried to will away a sense of helplessness that tempted him to go back to his bed and stay there until everything was over.

A knock on the doorframe startled him, and he looked up to see Eli standing in the doorway, holding a green plastic pot full of huge blooming yellow and orange mums.

"You okay?" Eli asked, scrutinizing Arden with obvious concern.

Arden couldn't help feeling a surge of longing as he looked at Eli. A part of him wanted to jump up and go running to Eli, and it took a lot of willpower to resist the impulse. He did push back his chair and stand up, as though that could do anything to close a distance between them that was more than physical.

"I'm fine," he replied, managing a halfhearted smile. "Is there something you needed? Julian isn't back yet, unfortunately, and I think Whimsy is meditating before trying to scry for your pack."

Eli's expression turned bashful as he approached Arden, holding out the flowers. "These are for you. Thought you might need something to help you feel better after yesterday. The pot ain't fancy, but I figured you'd like these better than cut flowers."

For a moment, Arden could only stare at Eli, completely gobsmacked. "You brought me flowers? Really?"

He wasn't sure if the uncertainty he felt was his own, or if it was something he was picking up on from Eli, but good manners came to his rescue. He stepped around his desk and walked toward Eli, the weight of doubt he'd been carrying around feeling lighter with every step he took. Stopping in front of Eli, he looked up into his beautiful eyes, and things somehow seemed a lot better.

"Thank you. They're lovely," he said, reaching out for the pot. "I love mums. How did you know?"

"I didn't," Eli said, a flash of relief crossing his face. "I went to a nursery instead of a florist, and they had mums all over the place. I thought these colors were pretty. I figured you might want something cheerful."

Arden was touched. "What a sweet thing for you to do," he replied. He looked down at the beautiful blooms and felt himself smiling for the first time in what felt like days.

"I'm glad you like them." Eli caught Arden's chin and rubbed his thumb lightly beneath Arden's smile. "I'm glad to see this too. Seems like I ain't done nothing but brought trouble to your life."

The touch of Eli's warm fingers sent an electric jolt through Arden, and he drew in a breath at the unexpected surge of need he felt. Whatever obstacles stood between them, something within him was trying to tell him that they were irrelevant, that he and Eli were meant to be together no matter what. But things weren't that simple, he reminded himself firmly. He couldn't get carried away, no matter how much he might want to.

"You can't help what's happened," he replied, his voice husky. "It's not like you wanted any of this."

"I didn't want any harm to come to my pack. *This,*" Eli said, gesturing back and forth between himself and Arden, "was unexpected. If I'm honest, I ain't sure I can say I don't want it. The wolf sure as hell does," he added with a wry smile.

Arden was so startled by the admission that he almost dropped the flowers, and he hastily turned to place them on his desk before facing Eli again. He searched Eli's face. "What changed? Yesterday you seemed determined to find reasons why it wouldn't work." The words weren't an accusation; he genuinely wanted to know if something had made Eli have a change of heart.

Eli turned his gaze to the floor, seeming lost in thought. When he met Arden's gaze again, his expression was pensive but open. "I felt how scared you were yesterday. I didn't think twice about holding you because I knew you needed me. Not Whimsy or Julian. Me. I had a talk with Tharn this morning too. He said what we've got is special because we ain't alike. There's something about us that completes the other like no one else could. It'd be stupid to walk away from that, right?"

"Tharn said that?" It was apparently a morning for surprises, but anything that meant Eli might not walk away from their bond was a good thing from Arden's point of view. Then he thought about it and nodded slowly. "I can believe that. My parents are different, of course, but their connection is very strong. Even though my father is human and doesn't experience a mating bond like my mother does, I've never doubted his deep devotion to her."

"But you feel it too, right?" Eli searched Arden's face intently. "This ain't one-sided?"

"No, it's definitely not one-sided," Arden replied. He might as well be completely honest, since Eli seemed open to talking about it for the first time. "I should have known when I saw your aura what it meant, but it never occurred to me. I just felt I *had* to help you, and I figured the physical attraction was natural because you're so gorgeous."

Eli's lips curved in a pleased smile at the compliment. "You're a right pretty little thing yourself."

Arden surprised himself by chuckling. "A pretty little thing, eh? Well, I guess that's better than you thinking I'd been beat with the ugly stick."

"With those big green eyes and delicate bones, you're definitely more pretty than handsome," Eli said, tracing Arden's jaw lightly with his forefinger. "Would it help if I said you're just about the prettiest thing I've ever seen?"

The gentle caress made Arden purr in appreciation, and he leaned into the touch. Somehow the light stroking felt better than almost anything else he could remember. "I think I can work with that."

Eli let his gaze roam over Arden's face, looking at him as if seeing him for the first time. "Ain't no ugly stick ever come near you," he said, his voice quiet and deep. "Your mouth looks like it was made for kissing."

All the oxygen seemed to suddenly depart Arden's lungs, and he stared up at Eli, unable to look away even if he'd wanted to. "You're my mate," he replied softly. "I guess that means it was made for you to kiss."

"I reckon it was." Eli cupped Arden's cheek in his palm. "Tharn reminded me of a lot of things. Helped me get my head on straight about our bond. You're mine now, and I'm yours. We'll be stronger together and nothing but miserable if we try to fight this."

"I'm definitely going to thank Tharn later." Arden felt anticipation building until he thought he was going to go crazy. "Right now, I'd rather find out if you taste as good as you look."

Eli's smile widened, and he slid his hand around to cradle the back of Arden's head. "You don't think we're moving too fast?" he asked, a teasing glint in his eyes.

"Thinking is overrated." Arden stepped closer to Eli, wrapping his arms around Eli's waist. "And this is the slowest damned 'moving fast' that ever happened. Are you going to kiss me, or am I going to have to have Whimsy hex you after all?"

"A bossy little thing too," Eli murmured, but he chuckled as he bent his head and claimed Arden's lips at last.

The tingle Arden experienced when Eli touched him was nothing when compared to the jolt he felt when their lips finally met. Nothing else in his long experience could have prepared him for the power and the pleasure of being kissed by his mate. He gasped, closing his eyes as he pressed closer to Eli, parting his lips in a silent demand for more.

A low growl rumbled in Eli's chest as he deepened the kiss, answering Arden's demand with one of his own for Arden's surrender. He slid his arm around Arden's waist, pulling Arden tight against his body as he plundered Arden's mouth, tasting and exploring.

The growl made Arden's knees go weak with need. Eli was his, and the *wolf* was his as well, and he wanted both sides of Eli's nature. He kissed Eli back, reveling in the strength of Eli's arms as he surrendered completely to whatever Eli wanted. Eli pushed Arden back against the desk and insinuated his hard thigh between Arden's legs, the growl growing louder and deeper. Eli tightened his fingers in Arden's hair, kissing him with a growing hunger that reverberated along their bond.

Arden was no stranger to passion, but what Eli made him feel was more intense, more *right* than anything he'd ever known. All he could think of was how much he needed Eli, how much he wanted Eli to claim him right then and there.

"I take it things have happened in my absence." A voice broke into the moment, a familiar deep baritone with a tone as dry as dust. "Or have you added a floor show?"

Arden moaned in denial, tightening his arms around Eli. As worried as he'd been about Julian, it figured his friend would pick the most inconvenient time in the history of inconvenient times to show back up.

Eli drew back slowly, seeming in no hurry to end the kiss, and he glared at Julian, his growl taking on a different note.

"Why? You like what you see?" he asked.

Julian raised a brow. "It's erotic as hell, so, yes, actually," he replied. "Feel free to continue if you'd like."

Arden was breathing hard, and he glared at Julian. It was probably a good thing he couldn't do magic the way Whimsy could, because he would have happily hexed the smirk off the vampire's face. "Damn it, Julian! You disappear for days, worrying us sick, and you show up *now?*"

"You don't appear very worried to me," Julian said, then put out a hand to support himself on the doorframe. It was quickly obvious despite his flippant response that he was exhausted, and he looked as though he'd lost weight in the two days he'd been gone. "I came back as soon as I could."

Eli released Arden with what seemed like reluctance, and he gestured for Julian to come in and sit down. "Did you run into trouble out there?"

"Not exactly." Julian didn't hesitate to take the invitation, and he dropped into a chair in front of the desk with a tired sigh. "There's a place far out in the mountains, where a friend of mine who had done a great deal of research into demons put his library for safekeeping. This was back seventy years or so ago, after the humans gained the ability to destroy the entire world at the push of a button." He glanced at Arden. "He was paranoid, like me, so there are a lot of wards to get through, and it took a lot out of me."

"I'm so sorry," Arden said, feeling a bit guilty for his uncharitable thoughts about his friend. He stepped away from Eli, trying to ignore the sense of loss he felt, and turned to the wet bar behind his desk. He poured a large glass of bourbon and brought it to Julian. "Especially since you seem to have been right."

"Oh?" Julian took the glass, downing the potent alcohol in a single gulp. "Did you find the possessed pack, then?"

"The what now?" Eli frowned in puzzlement at Julian.

Arden looked at Julian with a sense of dread. "Oh shit."

"If I'm right—and I'm pretty certain I am—we have a possessed pack of werewolves roaming around the area." Julian's lips twisted into a humorless smile. "I've been waiting for something like this to happen for the last twenty years or so. The Demon Time, as the folks around these parts call it, was somewhere around four hundred years or so ago. My mentor and sire—the vampire who turned me—arrived in this country not long after it happened, and so he witnessed the aftermath, not the actual events. But he was a scholar, and he developed a theory that incursions happen on a periodic basis. All he had were the oral teachings of the locals to go by, because the elves aren't native to this continent. But werewolves are, and it seems that whenever the demons are about to try to break through again, it's usually the wolf shifters or bear shifters they go after first, in order to raise an army. So when I heard that one pack had attacked another without provocation, killing some and taking the rest, it set off alarm bells."

"Aw, hell." Eli's face turned pale, and his eyes grew wide as he listened to Julian. "Is there any way to prove it? If they're possessed, can we help them?"

Julian shrugged. "Maybe, maybe not, since we don't know what kind of demon we're dealing with in the first place. Possession is tricky, and the longer the demon is in residence in the host body, the less of the soul that's left. It's fortunate that possessing a living body is so damned difficult in the first place, or we'd be in a lot of trouble. But if the demons are operating in the same way they have in the past according to the books, they could have been slowly possessing that pack for years. Once the first demon got in, it could bide its time, then gate in another to take over another body. I doubt that twenty or thirty demons capable of possessing mortal creatures popped in all at once—*someone* would have noticed, because the dark energy to do it would have been substantial. But one at a time, over a few decades? That wouldn't set off alarm bells until they began to act."

An icy fist of dread tightened around Arden's heart. "You know we went to see my father," he said, then glanced at Eli. "Unfinished business, remember? He kept saying that, that there was unfinished business."

"Sounds like they're looking to finish it," Eli said, reaching out to draw Arden close again as if he wanted the comfort of contact. "We got pictures from the settlement. They killed George—the alpha—and there was a glyph under his body. Does that mean anything to you?"

"Let me see." Julian's voice was harsh.

Arden pulled out his phone, pulled up the pictures, and then passed the device to Julian. The vampire scrolled through the pictures, then closed his eyes, as though the sight pained him.

"Let me guess—you started feeling really awful when you got close?" he asked, opening his eyes again and looking between Eli and Arden. Arden nodded slowly. "Please, please tell me you didn't touch or disturb anything."

"Not around the body," Eli replied. "I went to George's house and got the pack chronicle. I thought it might give us some idea about what happened. Other than that, we didn't touch nothing."

"Good. And yes, the chronicle might give us some insight into how they operate." Julian frowned. "I need to find a demon hunter. I could cleanse the glyph, but if I screw it up, I could bring something worse down on our heads. Right now, they probably don't know we're onto them. But that glyph means they've gated in a more powerful demon, so we're dealing with a possessed pack *and* something bigger. I'm going to have to try to identify that glyph. I brought some of the books back with me. I just hope I picked out one that can decipher that glyph."

"We can help you look," Eli said. "But what does all this mean for my pack? Are they gonna be possessed too?"

Julian nodded slowly, his expression sympathetic. "I would suspect that's why they were taken—to provide more hosts. Whatever the demon's after, it obviously feels it needs werewolves in order to get it. But it would take some time to gate in the demons to possess twenty werewolves, even with a higher-order demon helping out. Which is another reason to destroy that glyph—it will weaken the demon, maybe even send it back to the Abyss."

Arden bit his lip, pressing against Eli to offer what comfort he could by his presence. "It's only been a couple of days, so maybe most of Eli's pack is still all right. We need to get rid of that glyph as soon as we can."

"Yeah. We'll do what we can to help any that can be brought back," Julian replied, nodding to Eli in apparent sympathy. "But for that, we definitely need a demon hunter. I've never dealt with a possession before, and I'd hate it if I cast a living soul into oblivion by mistake."

"We ain't taking that kind of risk with my pack mates," Eli said, his brows snapping together. "I hope you know where we can find one. I don't know of any around Clayton. We ain't had much need of one."

"Yeah, I know where to find one." Julian's voice was flat. "The question is whether he'd help us or shoot us on sight."

Eli raised one eyebrow. "That don't sound very helpful to me."

"You mean Micah Carter? He's still alive?" Arden asked, and when Julian nodded, Arden turned to Eli. "He's got a reason for being the way he is. His son and his daughter-in-law were both demon hunters too. They're the ones I mentioned before, who were killed in a car accident about twenty years ago. Anyway, the old man washed his hands of all the supernaturals and retreated to his farm. We haven't needed him, and since he wants his privacy, we've left him alone. I think most people thought he was dead too."

Julian nodded. "Yeah, pretty much. I knew him better than most, because of my special interest in the soulless. I tried contacting him a few times, just to check on him, but he's rebuffed every overture." He shook his head. "I'm afraid we can't afford to give him an option this time. He's needed. Badly."

"Yeah, I understand how he feels, but we don't have a choice," Eli said. "How soon can we pay a call on him?"

"It's early. We can go today," Julian replied, then glanced sidelong at Arden. "Although I'm going to need to feed first."

Arden's eyes widened, and he glanced quickly at Eli. In the past, Arden would have immediately offered himself up to take care of Julian's need, but things were different now. He didn't even *want* to have Julian bite him, which might be a result of finding his mate. "Um… I'll call Whimsy, if that's all right. It's, um… well…."

"Arden is my mate," Eli said, sliding his arm around Arden's shoulders in a blatantly possessive display.

"*Mate?*" Julian asked, seeming stunned by the revelation. He looked between Eli and Arden, as though not quite able to believe it. "Really? The two of you?"

"Yes, really." Arden tipped his chin up, and he had to admit to feeling a bit smug that Eli was obviously staking a claim. "It was a surprise for both of us, too, but that's how these things happen sometimes. So if you don't mind, I'm off the menu, though I'm sure Whims will be more than happy to make up for it."

"Sorry," Eli said, although the smirk tugging at his lips made it clear he wasn't all that sorry.

Julian recovered, chuckling in amusement. "Oh, how the mighty have fallen," he said, though it was hard to tell if he was referring to Arden or Eli. "Fine, call Whims. I take it he knows about this? I always seem to miss out on the fun."

Arden rested his head against Eli for a moment, then drew out his cell phone. "Of course he knows," Arden said as he punched in the numbers. "I had to warn him not to get his hopes up about Eli, after all. He's my best friend, but I'd have to do something dire if he set his sights on my mate."

"He's right scary when he gets mad," Eli said dryly.

Arden laughed, then spoke into the phone. "Whims? Hey, the prodigal vampire has returned. He's hungry, if you feel like being a happy meal. Okay, see you soon, bye! He's on his way, Your Highness."

"Thanks," Julian replied, and he seemed sincere about it. "I'd just go over to the Rainbow Room, except that it's the wrong time of day, and we're in a hurry."

"Happy meal?" Eli gave Arden a quizzical look.

Arden felt himself flushing. "Well, you know what a vampire bite does, don't you? It's, um… very pleasurable. *Very*. So I was joking around one day and started calling Julian's hookups at the Rainbow Room 'happy meals.' He's happy, they're happy, everybody's happy, right?"

"Sounds like it," Eli said, although a note of uncertainty crept into his voice.

Arden turned toward him, wrapping both arms around his waist as he sensed Eli was fretting. "No, I won't miss it," he said, gazing up at Eli. "After that kiss, I can't wait to see what things between us will be like."

"Looks like we'll have to wait to find out," Eli said, glancing at Julian.

"Sorry about that." Julian flowed to his feet and brushed

past the two of them so that he could retrieve the bottle of bourbon from the bar. He refilled his glass, then raised it to the two of them. "To be honest, I'm very happy for the two of you. Vampires don't get mates, and I envy you the certainty you'll have in one another. I always figured that Arden would find a mate one day, even though not all half-elves do. But he's the loving type. He *needs* someone he can take care of."

Arden was surprised and touched at the observation, and he reached out with one hand to squeeze Julian's arm. "That's a nice thing for you to say. Thank you."

"What? Don't thank me!" Julian said, his eyes gleaming with mischief. "I'm the antisocial sort, so I'm just as glad you couldn't latch onto me and fuss me to death."

"From what everyone keeps telling me, Arden's got plenty of fussing to go around," Eli said. "When he's fussed over me all he can and he's got more fussing to do, I'll send him on over to you."

"Oh no! He's your problem now," Julian said, holding up his hands in denial. "See? We have to rescue your pack so that you can turn his excessive cuddling tendencies upon them when it gets to be too much for you."

"Fussing over other people is fine, but the cuddling is all mine," Eli said firmly, tightening his arm around Arden.

"We'll figure that out," Arden said. "We don't have to worry about it right now. We can talk about it after your pack is safe." He stroked Eli's back through the flannel of his shirt. "One thing at a time, right?"

"Yeah, we got enough on our plate right now," Eli said, seeming to relax beneath Arden's touch.

Eli apparently had a gift for understatement, and Julian rolled his eyes.

Whimsy arrived within a few minutes, and Arden and Eli left the office to give them privacy while Julian fed. Afterward, they decided that since the glyph had affected Whimsy so badly, it was better for him to wait at the resort and spend the time recovering and reading the pack journal they'd brought back from Georgia while Arden, Eli, and Julian dealt with the glyph.

They loaded up all the necessary supplies to cleanse the glyph in the back of Eli's truck—twenty fifty-pound bags of salt and enough holy water to fill a bathtub, as well as all the sage, cedar, and lavender they could find in the Asheville herbalist shop. Sadie, the human woman who ran the shop, had raised her eyebrows, but she knew enough about the local supernatural community to keep from asking questions. They also raided the tool shed at the Riverside for shovels, wheelbarrows, and other tools that might be of use.

They'd left the hardest acquisition for last; Julian warned them that Micah Carter was likely to send them packing, but they had to try to enlist his aid. There were many things that could go wrong, Julian had warned them, and having a bona fide demon hunter handling the cleansing was safer for everyone.

The Carter farm was far outside of Asheville, well away from the major highways and isolated from even the smaller nearby towns. But Julian didn't need a GPS to get there, and Arden rode shotgun in Eli's truck as Eli followed along behind Julian's SUV.

After a few minutes of riding silently at Eli's side, Arden scooted closer along the bench seat so that his leg pressed against Eli's.

"I hope Micah will agree to go with us," he said, putting a hand on Eli's thigh. "From what Julian said, he's gotten really bitter."

"I can understand why," Eli said, his thigh muscle tensing under Arden's palm.

Arden stroked Eli's leg, turning his head to smile at Eli. "I hope you don't mind me touching you. It feels good, even through clothes."

"No, I like it," Eli said, sliding one arm around Arden in return. "Maybe a little too much," he added wryly.

"I'm glad." Instead of sitting back where he had been, Arden tucked his legs up on the seat and leaned his head against Eli's arm. "I like the thought of having you at my side, and I do think we could make a really good team."

Eli was silent for a moment, and when he spoke, he sounded thoughtful. "Seems like we're meant to balance each other out in certain ways. Tharn says I'm too serious, and you can help with that, and I can keep you grounded." He paused, then slanted a teasing look at Arden. "And give you a convenient outlet for all your fussing and hovering."

Arden smiled unrepentantly. "I can't deny it. I like taking care of people. It's one reason I went into the hospitality business, I guess."

"It's a good fit for you." Eli went quiet again before adding, "We got some decisions to make when this is over."

Arden could sense the serious turn of Eli's thoughts. "Yeah, we do," he replied, stroking Eli's arm. "I know there will have to be compromises, and I'm fine with that. I want this to work, Eli. I want you. You're my mate, and I know we don't even know each other very well, but being with you is already important to me. Maybe more important than anything else has ever been."

"I want this to work too," Eli said, giving Arden a reassuring squeeze. "I had my doubts at first, but as long as we're honest, I think we can work out something that's fair for both of us."

"I'm sure we can." Arden smiled again, then widened his eyes. "I won't even resort to my secret weapon."

"Is that how you get your way?" Eli looked sidelong at

him, appearing amused. "You work folks over with those big green eyes of yours?"

"Why, is it working?" Arden asked, giving Eli a teasing smile. "I use whatever tool I need for the situation."

Eli gave a little snort. "I don't reckon it'd do me much good to pretend it ain't working. It don't seem fair, since I don't know how I can return the favor."

"Oh, I'm sure you'll think of something." Arden squeezed Eli's thigh. "When I saw you in that towel, I would have rolled over and bared my throat."

"Good to know," Eli said with a little smirk. "Maybe what's under the towel will work even better."

Arden drew in a breath, images rising up in his mind to torment him. He wasn't just flattering Eli by calling him sexy, and he was definitely anticipating what it would be like between them when Eli finally took him to bed.

His pleasant ruminations were cut short when the car ahead of them turned off the road and onto a dirt track with cornfields on both sides. They passed what seemed like miles of the fields before the track stopped in front of a house and barn.

The place seemed like something out of the nineteenth century, not one of the modern farms that had become commonplace. It made Arden feel almost nostalgic for how the world used to be, before supernaturals had become so jaded that they could worry about things like leash laws and pooper-scoopers.

Julian got out of his car, and Arden reluctantly pulled away from Eli. "I guess we should all be there, to show how serious this is," he said as he unfastened his seat belt. "We pretty much cover the supernatural spectrum between us."

They'd barely gotten out of the vehicles before the front door opened, and a man with thick white hair and stubbled cheeks barreled out of the house. He was dressed in overalls, a flannel shirt, and sturdy work boots, and he had a shotgun propped on his shoulder.

"I don't care who you are or why you're here," Micah Carter said, scowling at them from his vantage point on the top porch step. "Y'all can turn around and get on out of here right now."

Julian held up his hands. "Micah, it's me. Julian Schaden. I know you don't want to be disturbed, but we've come to you because you're the only one who can help us."

Arden took Eli's hand and moved up to stand beside Julian. He doubted the old man had more than birdshot in the gun, but he wasn't about to let Julian face it alone.

Micah peered at Julian with narrowed eyes, then gave a terse nod. "Julian," he said, a neutral greeting. "You've got the whole supernatural community in Asheville and Haywood County to call on. Seems to me you could handle anything that comes along without my help."

"Not a demon," Julian replied. He took a step closer. "We've got a problem, Micah. A possessed werewolf pack is running around. They've kidnapped another pack, and I'm pretty sure they gated in a higher-order demon."

"Shit," Micah said, drawing the word out to three syllables. "How sure are you it's demons and not something else at work?"

Julian turned to Arden. "Show him."

Arden nodded, taking out his cell phone and pulling up the picture of the alpha they'd taken. "We found this," he said, walking slowly toward the old man, not making any threatening moves. "Plus there was the feeling as we approached the area. Our friend Whimsy is a mage, and the aura of dark magic was so bad he couldn't go all the way there."

Micah propped the shotgun against the porch rail and fished a pair of glasses out of his pocket. His scowl deepened when he saw the photo of the glyph. "That's a demon's work, all right. Where did you find this?"

"In the woods near Clayton, Georgia." Eli stepped forward and addressed Micah. "The glyph was in the settlement of the pack that kidnapped mine. The alpha was dead, and the glyph was drawn beneath him."

"How did you avoid getting taken?" Micah reached for the shotgun again, scrutinizing Eli closely.

"I wasn't there when they attacked. I came home to find some of my pack mates dead and the rest gone," Eli said.

When Micah reached for the gun, Arden didn't even think; he stepped between Eli and Micah, shoulders tensing as he readied himself to grab for the gun if necessary. "He's my mate," Arden said, staring at Micah. "We've never met, but you'll know of my parents, Gilorean and Marin. I vouch for him."

Eli hooked his arm around Arden's waist, hoisted him up, moved him out of the line of fire, then stood in front of him. Micah gave an amused snort and left the gun where it was.

"You can't blame me for being suspicious of someone who escaped demon-possessed werewolves," Micah said. "I can't sense any taint on him, though."

Arden glanced at Eli, relaxing from the instinctive need to protect his mate from any threat. It hadn't been a conscious decision, and he smiled a bit sheepishly at how easily Eli had moved him out of the way.

"He's clean," Julian said. "But you see why we need your help. I don't know if I can cleanse a glyph that powerful by myself, and if I screw it up, they'll be able to trace it back to me. To Asheville."

"Grandpa?" A young man called out from inside the house. "Do you need any help out there?"

"No! Stay inside!" Micah's demeanor changed instantly.

"I'll loan you an artifact to help cleanse the glyph. That's the best I can do. I'll get it, and then y'all need to leave."

Julian's brows climbed, but he nodded. "All right. Thank you." He smiled rather grimly. "I suppose if I screw it up, you'll find out when the demons come calling around here, right?"

"Then don't screw it up," Micah said.

With that, he went back into the house. A few moments later, he emerged with a rectangular wooden box in his hands. "This is a feather from the wing of the angel that the Carters are descended from. You'll have to figure out which one of you is the most pure. I reckon that leaves you out, Schaden," he said as he offered the box to Julian. "Erase the glyph by tracing it backward with the feather. It'll absorb the evil from the glyph and from whoever's touching it. It'll return to the box on its own."

Julian looked taken aback as he accepted the box, and he held it almost reverently. "Are you sure you won't come with us?" he asked the old man somberly. "I appreciate you being willing to allow us to use this, but it almost seems wrong for it to be out of your hands."

"I've been out of this game for the past twenty years," Micah said, shaking his head. "I'm not getting back into it now. Whatever's going on is your problem to deal with."

"All right, then." Julian tucked the black box under his arm. "We'll bring it back."

"Keep it." Micah took a step back and raised both hands. "I've got no more use for it, but you might if more of those glyphs turn up."

Julian looked doubtful. "It's your family history, Micah! I'm sure your grandson...."

"You leave him the hell alone!" Micah strode up on the porch and grabbed his gun, and he shooed them away with it.

"He's got nothing to do with any of this, and he never will. Now get off my land!"

"All right." Julian backed away, not turning his back on the old man, as though afraid Micah might have a change of heart and shoot him in the back. When he reached Arden and Eli, he nodded grimly, then turned for his car.

Eli picked up Arden in a one-armed hold again, carried him to the truck, and opened the driver's side door. "Get on in before that old coot decides to put some extra holes in our hides," he said, a growl underlying his voice.

Arden didn't resist; he wasn't positive that Micah Carter was playing with a full deck, if he could threaten them just for asking for help. He scrambled across the seat and looked out the front window, watching as Julian got into the SUV.

"What in the name of the Most High is that old man's problem?" he asked, shaking his head. "I know he lost his family, but it was a long time ago, and it wasn't *our* fault! I thought demon hunters were absolutely dedicated about keeping demons in check. He didn't even seem to care!"

"Grief can make you do crazy things," Eli said quietly. "You heard the kid, right? Maybe Micah don't want his grandson put in harm's way. Maybe he can't stand to think about losing anyone else."

Arden looked at Eli, then moved over to press against him. "I can understand that," he said, knowing that Eli would probably have more sympathy for the old man because of his own situation. "But you can't protect someone all the time. Bad things are going to happen, and all you can do is try to be as strong as you can when you confront them."

Eli waited until Julian had backed up and turned around before doing the same. Once they were back on the paved road, he slid his arm around Arden's shoulders. "Yeah, I know. It ain't easy sometimes, that's all."

"I know." Arden relaxed against Eli, enjoying their closeness, glad that Eli had finally decided to accept their bond. "I keep thinking that if you had been there, with your pack, you'd be dead too. Or worse, you'd be possessed. I know it's horribly selfish, but I'm glad you weren't, because it sounds like nothing you could have done would have made a difference, and I would never have known you."

Eli was silent for a while, and then he gave Arden a little squeeze. "I've wished I'd been there with them more than once. Sometimes I convince myself I could've made a difference, but I know better. At least those demons ain't gonna be able to sneak around no more. We're onto them." He rubbed Arden's shoulder gently. "And I met you."

Arden smiled slightly. He was glad that Eli had finally accepted their relationship. Despite all they were facing, Arden felt a lot more confident now. What they had to do might be dangerous, but at least now it seemed that they would be facing it together—and that made it all seem much easier to bear.

CHAPTER 10

*E*li was glad when Micah Carter's farmhouse disappeared from sight in his rearview mirror. He sympathized with Micah to an extent, but it seemed grief had driven Micah to extremes. Besides, he didn't want to remain around anyone who pointed a gun at Arden.

He glanced down at Arden, who'd been nestled up against him during the entire ride back to Georgia. He hadn't thought twice about picking him up and putting himself in the line of fire instead, and he'd do it again. He'd never felt such a fierce sense of protectiveness before, not even for his pack mates. He'd always thought he would do anything for his pack if necessary, but he'd never been tested. Now he knew with utmost certainty that he would willingly die for Arden without hesitation.

He'd been dubious about Tharn's advice, but he had to admit Tharn was right. Once he made the decision to accept the bond, he found it easier to believe the situation wasn't as dire as he'd thought. The touching had definitely helped too. He'd never felt the kind of connection and desire he'd felt with Arden, and despite the ever-present concern he had about his pack, his thoughts kept turning to Arden. He wanted to get to know Arden and find out what they had in common to build a relationship on. He wanted to figure out what compromises they could make in order to build a life together. But most of all, he wanted to take Arden to bed and claim him as his mate. He wanted to make Arden his and erase all thoughts of Julian, Whimsy, Earl, and any other lovers from the past. For once, he and his wolf were in accord with their disappointment that claiming Arden would have to wait. They had a glyph to cleanse and Eli's pack to find first.

Instead of going to Eli's encampment, they went straight to the other pack's settlement. The body of the alpha was there, and not even scavengers had touched it, as if they sensed the evil tainting the area and stayed away.

"After we've cleansed the area, I want to bury him the proper way," Eli said, viewing George's body with more sympathy this time. If the demons had targeted his pack instead, it might have been him on that pole, and he owed a fellow alpha the respect of a formal burial.

"We can do that," Arden replied. He kept close to Eli and clasped his hand tightly as they stood together.

"Can and should," Julian added. His handsome face wore an uncharacteristically grim expression as he surveyed the scene. "Let's grab those wheelbarrows and start getting the salt spread. The sooner we get this finished, the happier we'll all be."

When they returned to the truck, Eli and Julian unloaded the wheelbarrows from the truck bed. Eli didn't have much interest in accumulating a lot of material things; he preferred to live simply. But he was also a Georgia boy, and his truck was sturdy and tricked-out—and probably worth more than his house and everything in it. But it had plenty of room for the salt, holy water, and wheelbarrows, and it was tough enough to handle the load.

Arden stood in the bed and helped with the bags of salt and barrels of holy water.

"I've removed a glyph or two in my time, but this is definitely a powerful one," Julian said. "I suspect the lower-order demons who are possessing the pack were gated in using animal sacrifices, so nothing that would be too noticeable in a forest as big as this one. Sacrificing a human, especially a supernatural human, ramps up the energy to cross between the lower realms and ours. You need it to pull in a more powerful demon."

"Do you think we can manage this one, even with an angel feather?" Arden asked. He wasn't pushing a wheelbarrow, but he had grabbed the shovels they needed for burying the alpha's body.

Julian smiled, but there was no humor in it. "We're going to have to hope so, I guess," he said, then shook his head. "Micah Carter has changed, that's for sure. The man I used to know wouldn't have handed over a family heirloom just to get out of cleansing a glyph. This is a major task for us, but it's what he was born to do."

Eli didn't know much about demon hunters, but he thought it was strange that Micah had run them off rather than doing his job. Maybe it was the pack mentality influencing him, but he thought it was each supernatural's duty to help in times of crisis—and this was definitely one of those times.

He and Julian covered the glyph with salt and holy water, and Eli thought perhaps the heaviness in the area seemed to lift a little bit once they were finished.

Julian was pale by the time they were done, as though the evil in the area was draining his energy. "Let's finish this," he said. He'd placed the black box with the angel's feather in it carefully to one side and had kept an eye on it while they'd worked, as though half-afraid it would disappear. Now he held it in his hands, seeming to hesitate.

"Micah seemed very specific about this," Julian said, looking between Eli and Arden. "He said that the purest among us must be the one to use it."

"Pure?" Arden blinked, looking at Julian, then casting a sidelong glance at Eli. "I don't think any of us qualify."

Julian shook his head. "Not physically pure. Spiritually."

"How does that work exactly?" Eli asked. "We gotta figure out which one of us has had the fewest impure thoughts?"

"Damned if I know," Julian said. "Maybe it will be obvious when we open the case. Are you two ready?"

Arden nodded. "Sure, I'm ready."

"Me too," Eli said.

Julian opened the case, and as he did, a beam of pure, dazzlingly white light flashed from it. For a moment they were all blinded, but then the light subsided slowly to an aura around the contents of the case. On a bed of deep red fabric lay a perfectly formed, pure white feather, glowing with energy. It was larger than a bird's feather, almost as long as Eli's forearm, which made sense if it had really come from the wing of an angel.

"Oh...." Arden's eyes were wide, and as Eli watched, the glow of the feather reached out toward Arden, bathing him in radiance until he appeared lit from within. His features seemed to change, becoming more ethereal, as though something of the spirit of the angel the feather had once belonged to was being transmitted to him.

Arden was pretty under normal circumstances, but now he looked beautiful, and Eli thought he was getting a glimpse at Arden's true self. He wasn't surprised Arden was the purest of them. Arden had shown his compassion and willingness to help others from the first time they met.

"Seems about right," he said.

"Me?" Arden focused on the feather, his expression of surprise becoming one of humility. He bowed his head for a moment, then straightened and reached for the feather. "I know what to do."

"Are you sure?" Julian didn't stop Arden from taking the feather, though he looked troubled. "Micah said you're supposed to—"

"—to trace the glyph with the feather, in the opposite direction from which it was drawn." Arden seemed very certain. "It was drawn counterclockwise, so I go clockwise. Don't ask me how I know. I just do."

"Er… well, okay. If you're certain," Julian replied, seeming a bit taken aback.

Arden smiled, then turned to look at Eli for a long moment. "You look even more beautiful than the first time I saw you," he said softly.

Eli cocked his head as he regarded Arden quizzically. "I should be saying that to you, not you to me."

"I see everything," Arden replied. "I see you as you really are, inside, and you're beautiful."

Julian snorted. "Well, if you can keep your mind on the task at hand, instead of on your mate, we can finish this business and go home so you can admire him all you want."

Arden laughed at that, then with obvious reluctance, turned toward the glyph. He drew in a breath and shivered. "It pulses with evil, like a foul heartbeat. It breathes corruption into our world, and we must stop it forever."

With that, he moved toward the glyph, touching the feather to the ground and walking around it clockwise. He traced the lines of the glyph, and as he did so, the lines of blood were drawn up into the feather, as though it was sucking the evil from the earth itself. The brightness never dimmed, and as the glyph disappeared, the oppressive feeling around them lessened.

When he finished with the glyph, Arden brushed the feather up the stake, then touched the body of the alpha. There was another bright flash, and the feather suddenly vanished. Arden stood for a moment, then slowly crumpled to the ground. Eli's heart lurched with fear as he rushed over to kneel beside Arden and gather him close.

"Arden?" He examined Arden swiftly, wondering if the feather had had unexpected side effects because Arden wasn't a demon hunter or a member of the Carter family.

But Arden's face was peaceful, and he opened his eyes, looking up at Eli with wonder. "It was like a glimpse of heaven," he said. "It took all the evil away, even the evil inside me."

"Hard to believe you had any evil in you," Eli said, smoothing Arden's hair back from his face with gentle fingers.

"We all have evil in us." Arden leaned into Eli's touch. "We can't help it. We're all mortals, no matter how long we live."

"He's right." Julian crossed to them, looking down at them with an unreadable expression. "The feather is back in the case, just like Micah told us. Wish he'd told us about the possibility of getting whammied like you did."

"I'm fine," Arden said, not seeming in any hurry to move from Eli's arms. "Really. I just felt really weak for a moment, but I'm better now."

"You just take it easy for a bit." Eli tightened his arms around Arden and stood up, cradling him against his chest. He carried Arden over to a hand-carved wood bench and set him down on it gently. "You sit right here. Me and Julian can handle burying George."

"All right." Arden smiled almost dreamily at him. "I think George is at rest now. The feather released his soul from being imprisoned in the glyph. I saw him go, and he seemed grateful."

Eli felt grateful as well to know George was at peace. The pack didn't deserve what had happened to them any more than Eli's pack had deserved their fate, and Eli put the blame on the demons, where it belonged.

"I'm glad," he said softly. "Thanks."

Arden leaned forward and kissed Eli lightly on the lips. "Bury him, and we can go home. The forest here is safe now."

Even though Eli wasn't sure if any werewolves would ever call this settlement home again, he was glad to know the area was safe for the dryads and anyone else who might inhabit it in the future. He stroked Arden's cheek with his forefinger and smiled slightly before he straightened.

"There's bound to be a graveyard nearby," he said to Julian as he went to get a shovel. "Most of us don't want to bother with human paperwork or risk discovery, so we bury our own."

"Over there," Julian said, pointing with his shovel toward the western side of the clearing. "I noticed it while you two were wrapped up in each other. Not that I was watching. Much."

"Course not," Eli said dryly. Julian appeared to have a voyeuristic streak, which perhaps explained why he'd enjoyed the company of both Arden and Whimsy.

He followed Julian over to the graveyard. It was smaller than the one at Eli's settlement, which dated back over three hundred years. They chose a spot for George, and between the two of them, they dug a deep grave quickly. By the time they finished burying George, Eli was sweaty, grimy, and tired. He was reminded too much of burying his own pack mates, and he was ready to leave this place and return to Asheville.

"Thanks for helping," he said as he and Julian tamped down the ground on George's grave. "I appreciate it."

"You're welcome." Julian brushed back his dark hair. Even though he wasn't sweating, he looked as tired and dirty as Eli felt. "Whimsy told me about the reception you got from those idiots on the council. I hope you've seen that Asheville is more than a bunch of effete paranormals buffing their nails while the world goes to hell around them."

Eli gave a quiet chuckle at Julian's assessment. He hadn't come away with a high opinion of the council, and obviously Julian shared that opinion.

"I have," he said. "I know who to go to when something needs to get done, that's for sure."

"Yeah. Some of us still give a damn about things outside of Asheville," Julian replied. Then he grinned and clapped Eli on the shoulder. "You're not so bad yourself, Hammond. Arden could have done a lot worse."

Eli snorted again. "Thanks. High praise indeed."

"From me, it is," Julian said dryly. "You'll get to know me, and I'll irritate you as much as I irritate everyone else. Which is fine, since most people irritate me too."

"Stop it, Julian," Arden scolded from the bench. "He's not that bad, Eli, really. But we can discuss this back in Asheville in more comfortable surroundings."

"Good idea." Eli gave Arden a stern look. "You stay right there. Me and Julian will get everything back in the truck, and I'll come back and get you."

"You'll carry me?" Arden widened his eyes. "Well, I guess I do feel a little weak still. I promise I'll be good."

"You better be," Eli said, wagging his forefinger at Arden and giving him a stern look.

Eli and Julian loaded up the shovels and the remaining salt and holy water into the back of his truck. When they returned, Arden was still sitting on the bench, and Eli examined him with a critical eye. He looked okay, but Eli wasn't willing to take any chances given Arden had used a magical artifact that wasn't attuned to him by blood or by type.

"I'm filthy," Eli said as he approached the bench. "But if you can handle a little dirt, I'd rather carry you to the truck."

Julian gave a huff of amusement, and Arden frowned at his friend before turning to Eli and holding out his arms. "I don't mind dirt. Unlike certain vampires who hate soiling their hands."

"They're dirty enough now," Julian replied mildly. He glanced around the empty settlement. "But we did a good thing. That's all that matters." With that, he dusted off his hands and turned to leave.

Eli scooped Arden up and held him close. He followed Julian, but he paused before leaving the settlement and looked around. This settlement wasn't his home, but it was close enough, and he wanted one last look in case he didn't return. Then he headed to the truck and settled Arden on the seat, handling him carefully as if he was made of porcelain.

Arden released Eli with obvious reluctance. "I like it when you hold me like that. It makes me feel safe and cherished."

"Ain't like you're a burden, Itty Bitty," Eli said, glancing sidelong at Julian and waiting for a smartass remark. "You don't weigh hardly nothing."

Julian shook his head but didn't comment on the byplay. "I don't think there's much more we can get done tonight, so I'm going to head back to my house and clean up, then see if Whimsy found anything in that journal. Shall we meet up tomorrow?"

"Sounds fine to me," Arden replied. He raised a brow at Eli. "Does that work for you?"

"Sure," Eli said. "See you tomorrow."

Julian nodded once, then turned and headed toward his SUV.

Arden watched him go, before fastening his seat belt. "I'm ready to go home. Unless you wanted to stop by your place? Now that the area is cleansed, it's probably safe for one night, at least."

Eli considered the idea, and he was tempted to suggest staying at his house overnight. But it wouldn't be the same without his pack there, and the place held too many unhappy memories now. He closed the passenger door, then moved around the truck to get into the driver's seat.

"Nah, I'd rather get on outta here," he said as he started the engine. "By home, do you mean the resort or somewhere else?"

Arden smiled. "Why don't we go to my house? You haven't seen it yet. And since you're my mate, it's technically now yours as well."

It wasn't Arden's *house* that Eli wanted to claim as his own, but he liked the idea of staying with Arden much better than spending the night in his cabin alone.

"Is that an invitation to spend the night?" he asked, reaching out to rest his hand on Arden's thigh.

"Yes." Arden put one hand on top of Eli's and gave it a squeeze. "I have a guest room, if you'd like, but my bed is also yours if you want it."

Eli brought Arden's hand to his lips and pressed a kiss to the palm. "I ain't staying in no guest room," he said, letting Arden hear the amorous growl in his voice.

Arden shivered slightly, but there was no mistaking the seductive smile he gave Eli. "Then I guess neither of us will be getting much sleep," he purred.

"I ain't planning on it." Eli bit down lightly on the heel of Arden's palm before releasing his hand. They still had a long way to go before they got back to Asheville, and Eli wanted a shower before they went to bed too, not just to wash off the dirt but also to wash away the residual taint he felt from that glyph.

Once they were on the highway, it was a straight shot back to Asheville, which Arden spent curled up against him as the sun slowly sank in the west. Arden directed him to skirt the city proper, then guided Eli to his exit, which was down a road that led through a stretch of pristine forest. The road crossed a small bridge, then turned south to parallel the French Broad River. After several minutes, an opening appeared in the trees.

"That's my drive," Arden said. "You can see it, of course, but it's hidden from normal humans."

They entered a copse of trees, and Arden pointed to the base of one huge oak. "There's my house. Just stop anywhere."

Eli pulled up close to the base of the tree and looked around, puzzled. "Where? Is it camouflaged?"

"Look close," Arden said. "There's a stair winding around the trunk." He grinned. "Or didn't I mention that I live in a treehouse?"

"You didn't mention that," Eli said, giving Arden an amused look as he got out of the truck.

"My bad." Arden took Eli's hand and led him to the stairs. "I hope you like it. I've gotten rather fond of living up high."

The stair was wide enough—barely—for Eli, but it rose gently rather than steeply. They ascended about thirty feet into the branches, then crossed a small rope-and-wood bridge to the house. The place didn't appear very large from the outside, but lights showed invitingly at the windows.

"Here we are. I call it the Aerie. The Faerie Aerie," Arden announced, trying to keep a straight face and failing.

Eli chuckled and shook his head. "Figures," he said, but he looked around with genuine admiration. "I reckon you've got a good view of the river?"

"I have a fabulous view of the river," Arden said. He opened the front door and gestured Eli inside. "Just go straight to the back of the room, and you'll see."

The main room was far larger than it looked on the outside, and it had an inviting circular shape. The back half of the room was floor-to-ceiling windows, with a set of glass doors in the center, which led off to a back porch. Arden's furnishings were minimal and looked as though they were designed for comfort rather than style. Even though Arden was small, his home was large enough to accommodate Eli's height and width.

Through the windows, there was a view of the wide, placid river, the shimmering water reflecting back the moonlight.

"Do you like it?" Arden asked, seeming anxious for Eli's approval.

Eli went to look out the windows, and then he turned back to Arden with a reassuring smile. "It's real nice," he said. "A lot nicer than my house. Better view too. I like being up so high. It feels safer."

Arden smiled, moving to wrap his arms around Eli's waist, then leaned back to look up at him. "That's what I thought. I've always felt safe in trees, like they'd protect me if anything happened. Even though this one doesn't have a dryad, there's plenty of them close by."

Eli slid his arms around Arden's shoulders, already feeling at home here. The house was aesthetically beautiful—exactly what Eli would expect from Arden—but it was comfortable and welcoming as well.

"Good to know. Seems like I feel some magic. You've got wards up too?"

"Well, it makes sense to be careful," Arden replied. "I don't want humans to see this place from the river. Not that I don't like humans, but they'd be too curious, and I don't want to have to explain this place. I can get by saying my ears are a birth defect, but my house is just a little too out of place for them."

"Makes sense." Eli smoothed his hands up and down Arden's back gently. "I like it."

Arden hugged him tightly, then stepped back. "Good. Why don't you shower while I make us something to eat? I'll find you a robe to wear while I clean your clothes. I might even have jeans and a shirt that will fit you, or at least a tunic. I've had a lot of visitors over the centuries, and things are always getting left behind."

"I don't need nothing more than a robe," Eli said, giving Arden a wolfish smile. "It's just gonna come off after supper."

Arden chuckled, giving him a wicked smile, then led him toward a pair of doors at one side of the big room. He opened the first, which proved to be a linen cabinet, and selected a big, fluffy towel and a folded robe in dark green. "Here you go. The bathroom is through that door there. I'd offer to stay and scrub your back, but we'd never get anything to eat, and I have a feeling we're going to need the sustenance."

"You've been with a werewolf before, ain't you?" Eli accepted the towel and robe, and then he bent to brush his lips against Arden's ear. "But you ain't been with an alpha," he murmured.

He heard Arden's swiftly indrawn breath. "No, not an alpha," he replied. Reaching up, he stroked Eli's cheek. "And not my mate."

"Better load up on protein," Eli said, and he gave Arden's earlobe a little nip before straightening up. "You'll need it."

Arden moaned softly, then looked up at Eli with wide eyes. "So will you," he replied. "Don't take too long." With that, he turned and walked away with a deliberately provocative sway of his hips.

Eli watched Arden go, thinking this would likely be the quickest shower of his life. Finally, he turned away and went into the bathroom. Arden's bathroom was almost as big as Eli's bedroom and bathroom combined at his house. The shower stall was spacious enough that even Eli wouldn't feel like he was in a cramped space, and it had massaging jets on the walls and a bench seat. The bathtub was separate, and Eli had never seen anything like it. It looked like a giant white bowl situated by a picture window overlooking the river, and water came down in rivulets from a fixture overhead as well as from a faucet. He'd never used a bathroom that fancy or expensive, but he thought he could get used to such luxury if he ended up staying in Asheville.

He showered and washed his hair quickly, using the shampoo and conditioner Arden had on hand. He towel-dried his hair and twisted it into a loose bun. Then he put on the robe and went to find Arden.

It was easy enough to locate the kitchen. Arden was singing softly in the Elvish language as he stirred a pot on the stove. Eli approached and slid his arms around Arden from behind, pressing close.

"Followed my nose to something that smelled delicious," he said, nuzzling the back of Arden's neck. "The food smells pretty good too."

Arden leaned back against him. "You smell pretty nice yourself," he replied, bending his head forward to give Eli better access. "I hope you're hungry. And that you want something to eat."

"I'm starving," Eli said, and he growled as he bit down lightly on Arden's neck. Arden gasped, and Eli could feel him shiver.

"So what do you want first? Me or the pork chops?"

"Like that's a real competition." Eli grasped Arden's hips

and pulled him snug against him. "If this wasn't our first time, I'd put you up on that counter and fuck you right now."

"You still could," Arden said, wriggling his ass against Eli. "But as it happens, there's a nice big bed less than twenty feet away that we can use."

"Then turn off the stove, and let's go," Eli said, his body already starting to tighten with arousal at the feel of Arden moving against him. He couldn't think about food with visions of Arden sprawled naked beneath him crowding his mind.

Arden pulled the pan off the burner and switched the stove off. He took one of Eli's hands in his and tugged him toward the doorway, seeming every bit as eager as Eli. "Good choice. I've been dying to see you naked since you greeted me in nothing but a towel."

Eli twined his fingers with Arden's and let himself be led to the bedroom. "Well, I ain't wearing nothing under this robe," he said, giving Arden a sly smile.

"You think I don't know that?" Arden asked, a heated gleam in his eyes. He opened a door, revealing a room with a king-sized bed. "So, will this do? Because if you don't fuck me in the next five minutes, I just might die."

A glance around showed Arden's bedroom was decorated in restful greens and blues, and his furniture looked to be sturdy but with a simple, classic design. The walls were lined with large picture windows, giving them an unobstructed view. But Eli was far more interested in the view right in front of him.

"What's an itty-bitty elf like you doing with such a big bed?" he teased as he followed Arden into the room.

"Maybe I somehow knew I was going to end up with a mate who could fill it," Arden replied. When he reached the edge of the bed, he turned to face Eli. "It's big enough to let us do anything we'd like. And what I want you to do right now is me."

"We'll get there." Eli closed the distance between them and smirked as he slid his hands beneath Arden's sweater, caressing the warm bare skin he found beneath. "But this is the first time I get to make love to my mate. I want it to be special."

Arden gave a soft moan as Eli stroked him, and he reached out to slide his hands into the opening of Eli's robe. "It will be, I have no doubt about that," he replied. "Because you're special. And you're all mine."

Eli sucked in a sharp breath at the strange tingle he felt, as he always did when they touched. It stoked his desire and made his skin hungry for more of his mate's touch.

"Do you feel that too?" he asked, splaying his hands on Arden's back. "The tingle?"

"Yes. It feels good." Arden combed his fingers through the hair on Eli's chest, then brushed his thumbs over Eli's nipples. "Do you like that?"

Eli slid his hands back around to Arden's chest and flicked his thumbs across Arden's nipples in return. "Yeah. Do you?" he asked with a teasing smile. He hadn't expected to feel like being playful while his pack was in danger. Perhaps he was too serious, as Tharn accused him of being, but Arden seemed to bring out a desire to tease and play.

Arden sucked in a sharp breath, and Eli could see a flush of desire rising on Arden's skin. "Yes! I like it a lot. I want more!"

"Then you need to get some clothes off." Eli pushed up the folds of Arden's sweater and helped him get it over his head. After Arden tossed the sweater aside, Eli let his gaze roam over his bare chest, admiring his lean build and wiry strength. The sight made him wonder if Arden really was stronger and sturdier than he thought. "Did Earl have to hold back?"

A teasing smile curved Arden's lips. "Are you asking me to kiss and tell, Mr. Hammond? If what you really want to know is if I can handle you, the answer is yes. I don't mind things getting rough—I enjoy it."

"Even werewolf rough?" Eli raised one eyebrow questioningly as he unfastened the fly of Arden's jeans, wanting to see more of his mate. "I reckon you're in for a lot of mending clothes in your future, then."

Arden chuckled, batting at Eli's hands. "I can do it faster," he said, before stripping out of his jeans and what looked like a pair of red silk boxers. He was already barefoot, so after he kicked the jeans aside, he stood in front of Eli, bare and aroused. "And you can rip my clothes off anytime you'd like."

"Give me the chance next time," Eli grumbled, but there wasn't any heat behind the words. He was far more interested in exploring Arden with his eyes and hands, and he couldn't resist curling his fingers around Arden's hard cock and giving it a teasing stroke. "Ain't nothing itty-bitty here."

Moaning softly, Arden grasped Eli's arms and tilted his head back. "I told you looks were deceiving."

The sight of Arden baring his throat—even if he wasn't doing it deliberately—called to the wolf, and Eli bent his head and ran his nose along Arden's neck, breathing in deeply of his mate's warm scent. He pressed his lips just beneath Arden's ear, then darted his tongue out for a little taste.

"Mine," he murmured against Arden's skin.

"All yours." Arden's voice was breathless, and he raised his hands, burying his fingers in Eli's hair and tugging it free of the knot. "My mate. My wolf."

The desire to bite Arden and mark his pretty, pale skin so the world would know he was claimed rose up strong, and

Eli couldn't resist nipping Arden's earlobe. "I wanna bite you. Wanna cover you with my marks all over."

"Yes! Do it!" Arden tugged on Eli's hair, and there was an edge of need in his voice. "I want your mark on me."

"Then you'll have it." Eli growled as he scooped Arden up in his arms and tossed him on the bed. He unfastened the sash at his waist and shrugged out of the bathrobe, letting it fall to the floor. Then he climbed onto the bed and crawled until he was braced over Arden, holding Arden's gaze as if he was stalking prey.

Arden stared up at him, his green eyes wide and dark with desire. Reaching up, he cupped Eli's cheek with one hand. "Please, Eli. I want you so much. I *need* you."

Eli nuzzled against Arden's palm, and he swooped down and fastened his teeth on Arden's neck, the need to mark his mate overwhelming in the face of Arden's desire. He breathed in the scent of arousal rolling off Arden's skin as he sucked and bit, and the wolf howled its satisfaction.

Crying out, Arden threw his head back and wrapped his arms around Eli's shoulders, clinging tightly to him. "Oh yes! Feels so good…."

Eli nuzzled and licked his way down Arden's throat to his nipples. He caught one tiny, hard nub between his teeth and tugged hard. Arden writhed beneath him, his skin growing hot and damp with sweat and desire. He raked his nails across Eli's shoulders, urging him on with whimpers of need. A steady growl of pleasure vibrated in Eli's chest as he mapped Arden's body, wanting to familiarize himself with every sensitive spot that gave Arden pleasure. He left another mark on Arden's inner thigh, and then he dragged his tongue along the underside of his cock and swirled it around the head, craving a taste.

"Oh God." Arden's voice was strangled, and he fisted his hands in sheets. "You're going to kill me. Don't stop!"

"Naw, I ain't letting you come yet." Eli braced himself over Arden and gave him a wicked smirk. "I wanna be deep inside you when that happens."

Arden released his death grip on the sheets, splaying his hands on Eli's chest, stroking Eli's skin and teasing his nipples. He licked his lips. "I want that too. More than anything."

Eli sat back and gazed down at Arden, unable to remember wanting any other lover as much as he wanted Arden. He'd never felt as if he needed someone's touch before, never felt such desperation to take and claim as he did now, and the wolf was urging him on.

"Get the lube," he said, "and tell me how you want me to fuck you."

Arden rolled to one side, reaching out to open the drawer in one of the nightstands. He fumbled around amid what looked like quite a collection of toys—including handcuffs and a rather large purple dildo—before he held up a bottle of lube. He handed it to Eli, then got up on his knees, grasping the headboard and looking back at Eli coyly. "How about like this? I want you to feel free to pound me as hard as you can."

Both Eli and the wolf liked that idea, and Eli didn't waste any time popping the cap open on the bottle. He coated his fingers generously with lube and positioned himself behind Arden. Grasping Arden's hip with one hand, he eased his forefinger into Arden slowly, making sure to stroke the sweet spot within.

With a gasp, Arden pushed back against Eli's finger. "You don't have to be gentle."

"Gotta make sure you're warmed up good," Eli said as he added a second finger and pushed it deep. "Then I won't be so gentle."

"Good." Arden bared his teeth in a wicked smile and

wriggled his ass enticingly. "I want you to pound me so I feel it for days."

Eli wanted that too, badly enough that it took all his willpower to add a third finger and make sure Arden was stretched and prepared. He leaned over and grabbed a tissue from the nightstand to wipe off his hands, which were shaking with his eager need to claim his mate. He retrieved the bottle of lube and poured out another generous amount so he could coat his cock thoroughly, and then he knelt behind Arden and smoothed his hands up and down the clean lines of Arden's back.

"My mate," he murmured as he slid one hand down to grasp Arden's hip.

Arden looked back at him with a smile that combined both desire and tenderness. "All yours," he said softly. "My Eli. My wolf. Complete our bond now, please!"

Eli guided himself into position and eased into Arden, forcing himself to go slowly at first. He didn't want to hurt Arden, and he also wanted to savor the pleasure of Arden's tight heat surrounding him, of claiming his mate for the first time. When he was buried deep, he grabbed Arden's hips and began to move.

"Yes!" Arden gripped the headboard of the bed, catching Eli's rhythm and moving with him with sinuous grace. "Feels so good. Feels perfect!"

It felt perfect to Eli too—*Arden* felt perfect. Eli's doubts faded in the wake of the overwhelming rightness of being joined with Arden, and the wolf rose up to give its blessing as their bond clicked into place, complete at last.

Growling, he slid one hand around Arden's body and curled his fingers around Arden's cock, stroking it hard and fast, wanting to feel his mate's pleasure reverberating along the bond, wanting to know his mate reached the pinnacle of ecstasy because of him.

Arden groaned as Eli stroked him, and Eli could feel his body tense as his arousal mounted higher and higher. Then Arden cried out Eli's name as he pushed forward into Eli's hand and shattered, a bright flash of pure, overwhelming joy radiating from him and into Eli as Arden came.

Eli's need threatened to spiral out of control, and he snarled as he grabbed Arden's hips, his fingers clenching hard enough to leave bruises. Arden was his now, and he let go as he claimed his mate with rough, powerful thrusts. Arden continued to move with him, reaching back over his shoulder to bury one hand in Eli's hair.

"Yes! I want to feel you come inside me," Arden moaned. "I want all of you."

Arden's continued pleasure stoked Eli's desire to a crest, and he bit down on Arden's shoulder as he surged deep one last time, swept away by ecstasy. Arden cried out again, arching back against Eli, their shared pleasure seeming to rebound back and forth between them in waves. The sensation faded slowly, until at last Arden slumped against him, resting his head back on Eli's shoulder as he gasped for breath.

"That was…." Arden seemed to have trouble finding a word, but then he sighed. "Perfect. Absolutely perfect."

Eli wound both arms around Arden and held him close, content to cradle Arden while they basked in the aftermath of their shared pleasure.

"Yeah, it was," he said, then pressed a kiss to the livid bite mark on Arden's shoulder.

Arden turned his head slightly, then gave a satisfied hum. "Too bad it's chilly out. I'd be tempted to run around without a shirt to show that off."

"Just as long as you know Julian ain't the only one who can bite you," Eli said, stroking Arden's stomach gently as he eased out at last. He regretted the separation, but he was ready to curl up with Arden and rest awhile.

Apparently Arden was too, because he turned so that he could push Eli down on the mattress, dropping down beside him and reaching for the covers that had gotten pushed back out of the way. He cuddled close, resting his head on Eli's shoulder and drawing the comforter up over them.

"You're the only one who gets to bite me from now on," he said, rubbing his cheek against Eli's shoulder like a contented kitten. "No one has ever made me feel like you do, and I know that no one else ever could."

"Damned right," Eli said with a drowsy chuckle as he gathered Arden close.

Now he understood what Tharn had been trying to tell him about the magic of the bond and the profound connection he would share with his mate. He hadn't believed it, but tonight had proven him wrong. Tharn would be delighted to learn he was right, but maybe if Eli bought him a beer or two or five, Tharn would let him live it down one day.

Maybe.

CHAPTER 11

*A*rden woke slowly, the warmth and contentment he felt letting him linger for a time in a state of peaceful drowsiness. He was aware of a big, warm body curled around him as though he were a stuffed animal, and he gave a soft hum of pleasure, feeling happier than he could ever remember being.

Eli was still deeply asleep; Arden could tell not only from the even cadence of Eli's breathing but from what he could feel along their bond. The connection between them was deeper now, and where he hadn't even been conscious of it at first, he could now seem to sense Eli's presence in a small, warm place within his mind. It felt comforting and right, a connection that promised he would never be alone again.

Smiling to himself, Arden thought about the perfection of the previous night. Consummating their bond had been an experience unlike anything else. He was no stranger to pleasure or desire, but what he and Eli had made everything else seem like a pale shadow. And it had only gotten better and stronger during the night, as they'd rested, then finally risen to eat before making love again. Much later they'd showered, then fallen into the big bed together, exhausted yet exhilarated. Arden hadn't ever given much thought to whether he wanted a mate or not, or if he'd even be capable of having one, but now that he had Eli, he couldn't imagine how he'd ever lived without him.

He opened his eyes, looking up at the ceiling of his bedroom, feeling Eli's warm breath stirring his hair. Turning his head, he looked into Eli's sleeping face, knowing that his smile was probably utterly besotted, but not caring very much. He had never been stingy with his affections by any means, but he'd also never been in love before. Maybe something inside of him had known he'd find Eli one day, and so his heart had stayed with him until Eli had come along to take it into his keeping.

Arden's peaceful idyll was shattered by loud banging on the doorframe.

"Wakey, wakey!" Whimsy singsonged at the top of his lungs. "Time to get up, young lovers!"

Arden flailed, startled, and bolted upright, staring at an evilly smiling Whimsy. Next to the mage, Julian was regarding Arden and Eli with a raised brow and more than a little interest.

"What in the hell?" Arden recovered enough to glare at his friends. "Who invited the two of you?"

Eli rolled onto his back, yawning, and knuckled his eyes. "This had better be real important," he said, a menacing growl underlying his words.

"It is, actually," Whimsy said, his evil smile fading. "We've been going over the pack chronicle, and we found some things of interest."

"Oh?" Part of Arden wanted to tell his friends to go away so that he could take Eli back to bed and keep the world and their problems at bay for a while longer, but he drew in a deep breath and nodded, knowing that anything that helped them find Eli's pack was important. "Let us get dressed, and we can discuss it. Would you mind putting on the coffee?"

Eli threw back the covers and rolled out of bed, not seeming to care that he was naked. Whimsy's dark eyes grew wide as he looked Eli up and down with grudging admiration.

"Yeah, sure." Whimsy cleared his throat. "Coffee."

"Got any clothes I can borrow?" Eli asked, his attention on Arden while he stretched leisurely. "Mine are dirty."

Arden gazed in admiration and felt a tingle of desire as he watched his mate. "Sure. There's bound to be something that will fit you."

"I know I left some jeans and a sweater here a while ago," Julian drawled. He looked over Eli's body with casual interest. "They ought to work well enough."

Arden raised a brow, feeling an uncharacteristic desire to tell Julian to keep his eyes to himself. It was an instinctive reaction, no doubt, because he knew Julian had no interest in bedding other dominant males, so Eli definitely wasn't his type.

"Would you mind getting them, please?" he asked, and was a bit chagrined when Julian gave him an amused look, as though well aware of the jealousy under Arden's careful politeness, before nodding and turning away.

"Got an extra toothbrush in the bathroom?" Eli asked. "Tell me where, and I'll get it."

"Yes, in the medicine cabinet," Arden replied. He pushed back the comforter. "We'll see about moving your things from the resort later today."

"Good, I'm ready to get settled in here," Eli said. "See y'all in the kitchen." With that, he sauntered into the bathroom.

Whimsy's jaw dropped slightly as he watched Eli go, but he closed it with a snap and crossed to Arden. "Holy shit, can you walk right? Do you need one of those doughnut cushions?"

Arden rose to his feet, giving Whimsy a smug smile. To be honest, he did feel a twinge from the vigorousness of their lovemaking, but it was a welcome reminder, not uncomfortable. He didn't even try to cover up the bite marks and bruises. "No, thanks, I'm fine, Whims."

Whimsy stroked the bite mark on Arden's shoulder lightly, a wry smile curving his lips. "Looks like you had a good time," he said, his voice soft with wistfulness.

"Yeah, I did." Arden impulsively reached out, hugging Whimsy hard. "I'm going to make it my personal mission to find your perfect romance, Whims. You deserve to be as happy as I am."

Whimsy wrapped his arms around Arden and held him tight. "I'm glad you're happy, I really am. You deserve it, and if that big lug ever dicks you around, I'll kick his ass."

Touched by Whimsy's words, Arden vowed to himself that he would do everything he could to help Whimsy find someone as wonderful as Eli. "Thanks, I appreciate that. I don't think you'll have to, though. I think all I'll have to do is turn the eyes on him."

"God help the poor man," Julian drawled. He held out a small pile of clothing. "He doesn't know what trouble he's in."

Arden rolled his eyes, stepping back from Whimsy and taking the clothes. "Like they ever worked on you," he said teasingly.

"You never needed to use them on me," Julian replied. He looked over the marks on Arden's body without comment, instead moving to drop an arm around Whimsy's shoulders. "Go on, get dressed. Let's get the coffee going, Whims. Maybe we can even make them toast, if I can remember how to do it."

"How can you not know how to make toast? Your kitchen

is nicer than mine," Whimsy grumbled as he let Julian lead him away.

Arden turned and headed to the bathroom. Eli was standing at the sink, twisting his hair up into a bun, and he watched for a moment, feeling a surge of possessive pride at the power and beauty of his mate's body. "Here's the clothing," he said finally, placing it down on the counter. Unable to stop himself, he reached out to caress Eli's back, savoring the feeling of silken skin over hard muscle.

Eli bent to give Arden a minty-fresh kiss, resting his hand at Arden's waist. "Thanks, Itty Bitty." He drew back, a heated gleam appearing in his eyes. "Too bad we got interrupted. I was looking forward to a round or two of morning sex."

"So was I," Arden admitted with a rueful smile. "But we'll have plenty of time for that—the rest of our lives. Maybe once we rescue your pack and everything is settled, we can take a honeymoon of sorts. We don't even have to go anywhere, just lock all the doors and turn off the phones so we can be alone."

"That sounds real good to me." Eli swatted Arden's ass playfully. "Now get on outta here and let me get dressed before I forget we have company and bend you over the counter."

Arden chuckled, turning back toward the bedroom, but as he walked away he swayed his hips enticingly, pleased when he was rewarded by Eli growling at him.

After dressing and taking a moment to brush his teeth as well, he and Eli walked into the kitchen. Julian was buttering toast under Whimsy's watchful gaze.

"All right, we're up and mostly conscious," he said, moving to the counter and retrieving two mugs from a cabinet. He filled them from the coffeemaker, then handed one to Eli. "What did you find that was important enough to risk pissing off an alpha werewolf?"

Julian snorted, then turned and placed two plates of toast on the island. "Sit and eat. If your mouths are full, you won't interrupt me."

Once Arden and Eli were settled to his satisfaction, Julian leaned against the island, looking at Eli intently. "Seems your fellow alpha had noticed some changes in his pack," he said. "Whimsy and I went over everything, trying to see if we could find a time when all this might have started. I'm not positive, but it looks like the first demon to hit that pack did it over a decade ago."

"How is that possible?" Eli said with a puzzled frown. "An alpha knows their pack. I can't believe George wouldn't have noticed something."

"He did, but he didn't have any reason to think it might be a demon," Julian replied. He shrugged. "The thing that caught my attention was something he mentioned where one of the young males, a kid named Jack, fell out of a tree and apparently was very severely injured. You shifters heal fast, but I guess this was bad enough that George didn't think the kid was going to survive. He did, but George mentioned that he thought, and I quote, 'Jack got his brains scrambled by that fall. He ain't been right since.'"

"You think a random demon got him while he was injured?" Arden asked. He took a sip of his coffee, mulling over what he knew of demons, most of which had been picked up by listening to Julian over the last hundred years.

"Maybe not random." Julian shrugged. "You know I was pretty sure a major incursion was imminent twenty years ago, which didn't happen, but there *was* more demon activity during that time. Before the Carters died in that accident, I was helping them try to track the manifestations and wipe up the low-level entities that had gated in. Maybe we missed one, and it took off for Georgia. If it found a place to hole up, it could have been watching that pack for years, waiting for one of the shifters to be weakened enough for it to possess him."

"Okay, I can see George blaming a fall on the boy acting differently, but what about the others?" Eli finished off his toast and swiped his finger across the plate to pick up some crumbs.

Whimsy slid off his seat and started rummaging in Arden's fridge. Arden pushed his own plate of toast over to Eli, but he wanted to hear what else Julian had found.

"Demons, even the low-level ones that aren't exactly the sharpest tacks in the box, can still be very cunning. George started relating over time that the young males in the pack were rowdier than usual, talking back to him more, but it wasn't anything he felt he could punish them for. I figure the first demon took over Jack, then at some point managed to gate in another. The second one would probably have had an easier time finding a host, if Jack was helping. Severe inebriation, a blow to the head, something like that, and now there are two possessed werewolves. It seems like my earlier speculation was correct—it took a long time, and because the changes were so slow, I don't think George caught on to what was happening. Not until six months or so ago, when he started feeling very uneasy about the way his pack was watching him. The last entry in the chronicle has him thinking about going to your pack for help, because he said his mate suddenly 'felt wrong.' She was probably the last one possessed, and it got to him through their bond."

While Julian spoke, Whimsy gathered up eggs, bacon, cheese, and other ingredients and began making omelets. Soon the kitchen was filled with the savory scent of frying bacon.

"But then it was too late," Eli said, his voice soft and filled with sympathy. "Is there a way to bring them back?"

Julian frowned. "I'm thinking that for the ones whose

souls haven't been completely obliterated, we might be able to use the feather. Micah said it removes the evil from whatever it touches, right? I can't imagine a demon being able to resist that kind of power, especially not the low-levels. We might run into problems if the bigger nasty they've gated in possessed someone. I still haven't found a match for that glyph, so I don't have a name or purpose for it."

Arden put a hand on Eli's leg and gave it a squeeze. "Surely any members of your pack should be able to be brought back by the feather if they've been possessed. If Julian's right, we just need to find them."

"That's the problem, ain't it?" Eli curled his fingers around Arden's and held on tight. "Ain't no telling where they got off to."

"It couldn't have been that far," Whimsy said, pointing at Eli with his spatula. "That's a lot of werewolves to keep track of, and some of them were probably wounded, which would slow down the whole group. Maybe it's time to round up a search party and start combing the area around Clayton."

Arden nodded. "We could do that. And I think I should go visit my father again." He grimaced. "I hate to ask him, but at this point, it's really important to know if he's seen anything else. If he can give us any hints at all, it would make all this a lot easier."

"I think that's a good idea," Julian said. "That 'unfinished business' thing has me worried. If we could figure out what their ultimate goal is, we can try to nip it in the bud before things escalate even further."

"Tharn and his pack will help search, I'm sure," Eli said. "I can go ask him."

"I've got a couple of friends who might help. I'll take the stuff I got from your settlement, and we can do a scrying together," Whimsy said, setting a plate with a large omelet and several slices of bacon on it in front of Eli, who eyed it dubiously.

"This ain't cursed, is it?"

"If I was going to curse you, I wouldn't mess up perfectly good food to do it," Whimsy said with a haughty sniff.

"A last meal, then?"

"Pfft!" Whimsy leaned over the counter and punched Eli's arm. Eli smiled slightly before picking up his fork and digging in.

Despite the seriousness of their discussion, Arden was very pleased to see Whimsy and Eli getting along. He smiled gratefully at Whimsy. It would have been very hard if his best friend hadn't decided to accept Eli, because Arden didn't want to lose Whimsy from his life.

"So it sounds like we have a plan for today," he said, filching a piece of bacon from Eli's plate. "Eli can go see Tharn. I'll go see my father, Whimsy can touch base with the other wizards, and… what about you, Julian?"

Julian smiled grimly. "I think I'm going to have to try Micah one more time," he said. "I know he said he's out of this, but I want to try to convince him it's still his fight, because he can do more by himself than all of us combined. His behavior has me really worried. It's like an elf standing by and letting a forest burn."

"Good luck with that," Eli said dryly.

Personally, Arden agreed with Eli, but he knew Julian, and Julian simply wasn't the type who could give up. If Micah Carter didn't end up helping them, it wouldn't be because Julian hadn't done everything in his power to convince the old man to do his duty.

"What about the council?" he asked, though he knew there wasn't much chance of getting help from that quarter. "Should we at least tell them what's going on?"

Julian gave a bark of laughter. "Why, so they can wring

their hands and say it isn't their problem? No, I don't think the council would do a thing. They laughed at me before, saying I was too paranoid. Do you really think they'd listen to me now?"

"No, I guess not." Arden huffed, annoyed again that the council wasn't more effective. "We could at least appeal to the witches. Do you remember the one at the council meeting, Eli? The one who was in favor of helping? Brianna's good. She isn't like the rest of them."

"I suppose." Julian shrugged. "If I strike out with Micah, I'll see if I can get Brianna and her coven to help." He straightened. "I guess I'd better get on it."

Julian rounded the island, stopping next to Eli for a moment. "Tell Tharn about the chronicle, and make sure that if he has any suspicions about any members of his own pack, he needs to do something."

With that, Julian nodded to them all and left. Arden watched him, biting his lip. He hoped Julian had luck convincing Micah to help, because the thought of the four of them going up against twenty or so demons was more than a little daunting.

He looked at Eli, seeing the strength of his mate, and he couldn't help leaning in and wrapping his arms around Eli, taking comfort in his warmth and closeness. He wished they didn't have to face so much just after consummating their bond, but there wasn't much to be done about it. He fought down a sense of foreboding, telling himself that nothing was going to happen to Eli if he was out of his sight for a few hours. Eli was just going to see Tharn, and then they'd be together again.

Eli slid his arms around Arden in return and rubbed his back soothingly. "Don't worry, Itty Bitty. We'll work together, and everything'll be okay."

"I know. I was just thinking that I couldn't bear for

anything to happen to you," Arden said, holding on to Eli tightly. Then his own words reminded him of something, and he chuckled, reaching into the pocket of his robe. "With everything going on, I almost forgot. I picked this up at your house. I meant to give it back to you." He pulled out the little carved wolf figure and held it up. "Here. You should finish it."

Eli took the wolf, regarded Arden with surprise. "Why'd you pick this up?"

"I don't know, really," Arden replied slowly. "I thought it was pretty. And it made me realize there was a lot about you I needed to learn. That I wanted to learn about."

Eli's expression softened. His blue eyes grew warm as he put the wolf back in Arden's hand and curled Arden's fingers around it. "Keep it. After this mess is over, I'll finish it for you."

"Really?" Arden smiled, absurdly touched by the gesture. "Thank you." He leaned in and kissed Eli, taking his time about it, not even stopping when Whimsy gave a snort of amusement and began to serenade them with a rendition of "Love is a Many-Splendored Thing."

For some reason, it made him feel better to have a piece of Eli he could hold on to. It was probably silly and romantic, but Arden didn't care. For the first time in his long life, he was in love, and despite the less-than-ideal circumstances, he was going to enjoy it while he could.

CHAPTER 12

"It's good to see you, my son."

"Thank you, Amma." Arden kissed his mother on the cheek, then entered the house as she stepped back. For once she didn't seem to have known he was coming, which was both unusual and a bit disturbing. It had been a running joke in their family for years that trying to surprise his father was a fruitless endeavor. "Is Appa all right?"

Marin nodded, though Arden saw the worry in her eyes, a change from her normal serenity. "He's been preoccupied for the last few days. Since your last visit, he's been trying to delve into the uncertainty surrounding his vision. It concerns him that you and your mate are involved and yet he cannot see clearly."

Arden took his mother's hands in his and squeezed them. "We have a plan to find Eli's pack and deal with the demon," he told her, hoping to reassure her despite his own concern about the situation. "Can I see him?"

Marin searched his face, then returned the pressure of his hands before releasing them, a slight smile curving her lips. "Of course you may. And I am glad to see that you and your mate overcame the distance between you. You deserve to be happy, Arden. And so does your Eli."

Touched, Arden leaned in to kiss her cheek again. "Thank you, Amma. I will find you after I talk to Appa."

She nodded, and Arden headed toward the stairs leading down to his father's study. Gilorean was seated at his worktable, bent over a large quartz crystal and staring into its depths as though mesmerized.

"Appa?" Arden spoke softly, almost afraid to intrude lest he break into a vision.

For a moment Gilorean didn't answer, but then he looked up, blinking rapidly for a moment. "Arden. I knew you would come. Though the future refuses to resolve itself, this part I could see."

There were lines of strain on Gilorean's face, and Arden hurried to his father's side. "Appa, you shouldn't focus for so long. If it won't become clear, you can't will it to become so."

"I know, I know." Gilorean pinched the bridge of his nose. "Don't try to teach your father his own craft, Sprout."

Arden smiled at the nickname Gilorean had called him when he was a child, but then he sobered. "If you knew I would come, you know why I'm here. Even if you haven't seen clearly, is there anything at all you know that we could use? The name of the demon, perhaps? Where he might be hiding, even if it's not completely certain?"

Gilorean looked at Arden, and his faded green eyes—once just as bright as Arden's own—were troubled. "Nothing clear. I get the feeling of south, and yet somehow... north and west. There is a pull from both directions, like a compass needle caught between two poles. Both are an answer. It is the question which is unclear."

"South... we're pretty sure the pack is to the south," Arden murmured, trying to make sense of Gilorean's words. "I have no idea what could be to the northwest.

That's the Qualla reservation. And the mountains, of course."

Suddenly Gilorean clutched Arden's arms, his eyes almost rolling back in his head. "The souls of the dead are in the mountains, they fly on the wind! I hear them singing songs of destruction in their stolen voices. They cannot live, they cannot die, and they cry out to the darkness to end their torment!"

With that, Gilorean slumped forward, and Arden caught him, lowering him to the ground. Heart pounding, Arden called out for his mother, then checked to make sure his father was still breathing.

Marin appeared in a rustle of skirts and knelt down beside Arden. "I feared this might happen," she said, and Arden noticed that she had a bottle and spoon in her hands. She measured out a dose of the tincture. "Hold his head up. That's right."

She poured the liquid carefully into Gilorean's mouth, and Arden felt him swallow reflexively. Within a minute or so Gilorean's eyelids fluttered, and then he looked up at them. Arden sagged with relief.

"Help me get him up to bed," Marin instructed. Between the two of them, with what help Gilorean himself could provide, they got him up to the bedroom and tucked between the covers.

Gilorean was very pale, and he closed his eyes as soon as he was in bed. Marin brushed a hand over his forehead, then nodded to Arden, gesturing to the door.

Once they were in the living area, Arden turned to his mother. "How much more of this can he take?" he asked, his voice rough. He didn't want to lose his father. Even though wizards lived much longer than normal humans, he knew Gilorean was extremely old.

"I do not know." Marin clasped her hands together. "The

peace of the past few years has been a blessing because there have been fewer unexpected visions, and I haven't allowed many people to trouble him with questions. But the last week or so, there has been nothing I can do."

Arden bit his lip, trying to figure out what could be done. "Maybe if we can get rid of the demon, the bad visions will stop."

"Perhaps." Marin sighed and reached out to touch Arden's cheek. "I am going to have some friends put wards around the house to dampen down the magic. I hate to do it, but I don't want to risk your father's health. You understand, don't you, Arden? These visions are too much for him."

Looking into his mother's eyes, seeing the worry for her mate, Arden did understand. He would do the same if Eli were in danger because the thought of losing his mate was beyond horrible. "Of course I do," he said. "Do it, Amma. Protect Father, and I'll do everything I can to help stop the visions at the source."

"Thank you." Marin kissed Arden's cheek. "Go on, then, and get back to your mate. Give him my love, and when this is all over, we'll have a real family meal together."

"I'd like that." Arden smiled, kissed his mother, and headed toward the door. "Let me know if you need Whimsy to help with the antimagic wards. He's good with that kind of thing."

"I will. Be safe, my son."

Arden gave her a playful grin as he left the house, then closed the door carefully after himself before heading down the path into the forest. He wanted to call Eli, but he knew there wouldn't be any cell phone reception this deep in the woods, so he settled for hurrying back toward the car so he could tell Eli what his father had said.

The part about the mountains and the voices of the dead didn't make much sense, unless it had something to do with the "unfinished business" his father had mentioned during his first vision. It almost sounded like there was something haunting the mountains, but ghosts didn't tend to hold any interest for demons, or at least not from what Arden remembered. Demons mostly wanted to create fear and trouble, spreading their evil in the world as an extension of the will of the Unholy. Many types consumed the bodies of the dead for sustenance while they moved about the world, but the higher-order ones drew their power directly from the Unholy itself. That was why getting rid of the glyph had been important, to weaken the demon who'd been summoned through it.

Arden continued walking as he tried to make sense of the seemingly unrelated information. He was so preoccupied with his thoughts that it took him a few minutes to realize that the only sound he could hear was his own footsteps. He stopped, confused by the lack of the usual forest sounds. No wind stirred the bare branches of the trees, nor were there any sounds of animals or birds. Everything was utterly still, and the hairs on the back of Arden's neck rose suddenly as his quirky intuition finally alerted him to the fact that something was very, very wrong.

Then the first massive wolf stepped out from behind one of the trees, and Arden knew without a doubt that they weren't going to have to go looking for the possessed pack anymore—the pack had come looking for him.

CHAPTER 13

"**G**eorge figured it out too late, and—" Eli froze midsentence as a wild fear that bordered on panic surged through him, and he knew with absolute certainty that something had happened to Arden.

"Something wrong, boy?" Tharn peered at him with concern. They were in Tharn's parlor, where Eli had been filling in Tharn on what they had learned from George's pack chronicle. But all thoughts of the chronicle fled as a fear that was entirely Eli's own rose up.

"Arden," Eli said hoarsely. "Something's happened."

"What's wrong?" Tharn asked, rising to his feet. "You feel him? Is he hurt?"

"He's scared," Eli said, unable to sit still any longer. He stood up and began to pace. "Almost panicky. He went to see his dad. Maybe something happened to his dad?"

"Maybe." Tharn put a hand on Eli's shoulder. "Concentrate. Try to reassure him. If he can feel you there, it might help him."

Eli drew in a deep breath and focused on Arden, trying to send calm reassurance along their bond. He had no idea if he was doing it right, but he wanted to help Arden any way he could until he could find out what was going on. But the fear he felt from Arden escalated to terror, and Eli started to doubt this had anything to do with Gilorean. Suddenly, the panic and fear cut off abruptly as if a wall had slammed down—or the bond had been severed.

"It's gone!" Eli whirled to face Tharn, clutching his chest with one hand. "I can't feel him anymore!"

"Gone?" Tharn frowned. "Breathe deep, boy. Gone how? He passed out? I know he ain't dead or you'd be out cold yourself."

"No, he ain't *there*," Eli said, rubbing his chest as if he could soothe the empty place he felt inside somehow. "It feels like the bond's been cut."

"It can't *be* cut!" Tharn scowled. "Unless… it could be magic, maybe. Something interfering between you and him. If he was scared, there must have been a damned good reason."

"I've gotta find him," Eli said, pulling out his phone. "I'll call Whimsy. He knows where Arden's folks live. We'll start there."

"All right. I'll get the boys together, and we'll go with you." Tharn looked grim. "Whatever happened, we'll find your mate and deal with it."

Once Eli got on the phone with Whimsy, things started happening quickly, but not quickly enough to satisfy him. He felt Arden's absence like a gaping void, and the thought of spending the rest of his life like that terrified him. Arden *had* to be all right. They had only just found each other and solidified their bond. Eli couldn't bear to think about losing him already.

When Whimsy arrived at Tharn's settlement, Julian was with him.

"I called him as soon as I got off the phone with you,"

Whimsy explained, his dark eyes filled with worry. "I figured we could use all the help we can get."

Julian looked grim. "We'll find him, no matter what we have to do. Or who we have to kill."

A few minutes later, they were on the road to Arden's parents' house. Tharn and his pack, including the fierce Morag, followed behind Eli's truck and Julian's SUV. Whimsy rode with Eli and gave him directions.

"We didn't have any luck with the scrying," Whimsy said, giving Eli an apologetic look. "I got some help from the best scryers I know, but there was something blocking the view with every item we tried."

"It was worth a shot," Eli said.

When they arrived at the house, Eli, Whimsy, and Julian went to find Marin while Tharn and his pack waited.

Marin looked troubled when she answered the door, and she grew pale as she looked at Eli and the others. "Something's happened, hasn't it?" she asked. She held out a shaking hand to Eli. "Where is my son?"

Eli clasped her hand and squeezed it, wanting to receive comfort as well as offer it. "I was hoping you could tell us. Was he here?"

"Yes. He came to see Gilorean. My husband had another vision, and Arden was concerned." Marin closed her eyes briefly. "He left, saying he was going back to you. I told him to be safe."

"I felt him," Eli said. "He was scared, and then I couldn't feel him at all."

Marin's hand tightened on Eli's. "You think he was attacked? Here in the forest?"

"That's what it looks like." Despite his own fears, Eli wanted to offer some solace, hating to give Marin a reason to worry about her son as well as her husband. "But I got Tharn and his pack to help us look. We'll find him."

"I'll help you." Marin drew in a breath. "I know the shortcut Arden takes when he's alone."

"I'll get Tharn and a couple of other werewolves who know his scent," Eli said, releasing her hand with one last squeeze. "We'll track him."

Marin nodded, then stepped outside. She took a moment to hug Whimsy and Julian, seeming to take comfort from having Arden's friends there, then moved off toward the forest.

Rather than the path Whimsy had led them along, Marin headed with assurance directly into the trees. There was no marked path, but she seemed to know exactly where she was going. Eli veered off to get Tharn, Morag, Earl, Rick, Paul, and Daryl, who were all familiar with Arden's scent. They all transformed and loped through the trees to catch up with Marin.

Even before they reached Marin, Eli picked up Arden's scent, and he howled to gather the others to him. They followed the trail, which was mixed with other familiar scents, at least to Eli. A ball of ice formed in his belly at the confirmation that Arden had been kidnapped by members of George's pack, although he couldn't figure out why they wanted Arden. It would make more sense for them to target Eli instead.

The leaves on the floor of the forest and the tracks told a grim story. It was obvious that the werewolves had toyed with Arden, chasing him, herding him, even, which would explain the terror Eli had felt coming from his mate. Arden had backed up against a tree, and there was a scent of blood where Arden had obviously tried to scramble up and had likely scraped his hands as they'd dragged him back down.

From there, the trail led back in the direction of the road into the forest. But then the trail went cold, the scents of Arden and the possessed werewolves replaced by gas, oil, and rubber. Eli sat on the cold ground, threw back his head, and howled out his anguish. They were right back where they started: Arden was gone, and Eli had no idea where or how to find him.

Whimsy and Marin both came to him, wrapping their arms around him to comfort him and share in his pain.

"We'll find him," Whimsy said, an edge of anger to his voice. "I promise you that."

Eli was grateful to have something almost like a pack to draw strength and comfort from. He wasn't cut out to be a lone wolf, and he couldn't possibly find Arden by himself. After a minute or two, he backed out of the embrace and transformed, gazing at them bleakly.

"How? Those possessed werewolves got him, and you said scrying ain't working on them."

"I have an idea."

Eli turned to see Julian walking toward them. The vampire had stayed behind at the site where Arden had been attacked, though Eli hadn't paid much attention at the time. He had something in his hand, and when he held it up, Eli could see bits of tree bark—the bark that had Arden's blood on it.

Whimsy smiled grimly. "I think I know where you're going with this. Blood magic, right?" Julian nodded, then Whimsy suddenly looked excited. He turned to Eli. "That wolf figure you gave Arden, the one you carved? Did you happen to cut yourself while working on it? Maybe get a bit of your blood on it?"

"There's nary a finished piece that *don't* have my blood on it," Eli said, hardly daring to let himself indulge a faint flare of hope.

"Perfect." Whimsy reached into a pocket of his robe and pulled out a snow-white handkerchief. He opened it up. "Put the bark in here. Marin, can I borrow some supplies from Gilorean?"

"Of course."

With Tharn and his pack trailing along behind them, on guard for any unexpected dangers, they started back toward Marin's home. As they walked, Whimsy explained what he had in mind.

"The scrying didn't work, but while there is a tie between someone and their possessions, it isn't anywhere close to being as strong as that between someone and their own blood. They have Arden, and we have some of his blood. You're with us, but Arden has something that has your blood on it. I'm hoping that with that kind of double linkage, we can home in on his location, and the blood magic will lead us right to him."

"If you need more of my blood, I'll gladly give it," Eli said. He didn't care what it took to get Arden back.

"I don't think that will be necessary," Whimsy replied. "Let's just hope the spell works."

When they reached Marin's house, Whimsy asked Eli to make a small fire, then went inside with Marin. He came back before long, holding a small copper cauldron filled with water, and Marin trailed behind him, carrying a basket filled with various herbs and other items.

Tharn and Morag had helped Eli gather dead branches and rocks to make a fire pit, well back from any of the trees. By the time Whimsy returned, they had a small, bright blaze going.

Marin took a metal tripod out of the basket and placed it over the fire. There was a chain hanging from the apex, with a metal hook from which Whimsy hung the copper cauldron. As the water began to heat, Whimsy pulled out a wand, tracing magical symbols in the air as he slowly added various bits of herbs to the water and chanted in the language of magic.

Eli stood back, watching without understanding much of what Whimsy was doing. He'd had minimal exposure to wizards or witches since his pack had tended to keep to itself, and there wasn't a local community like the one in Asheville. But it was reassuring that Whimsy seemed to know what he was about, his movements graceful and assured as he wove the spell. The air around them seemed to change, humming with a sort of unseen energy that made the hairs on Eli's neck stand up.

There was steam rising from the water, and Whimsy beckoned Eli to come forward. Eli moved closer, regarding Whimsy curiously.

"Give me your hand," Whimsy said, holding out one of his own. "I'm going to take a little blood."

Eli placed his hand in Whimsy's, palm up, without hesitation. "Whatever you need. I want to get Arden away from those demons as soon as possible."

"We will." Whimsy gestured with his wand across Eli's palm. Eli felt a tingle of magic, but no pain as a line of blood welled up on his skin. Whimsy held Eli's hand over the cauldron, tipping it to the side so the blood dripped into the water. "That should be enough."

When Whimsy released his hand, Eli was surprised to see that there was no trace of blood, and not even a mark on his skin. But Whimsy's attention was back on the spell, as he watched the water in the cauldron change from clear to a deep red.

After pulling out the handkerchief, Whimsy added the bits of bark to the water, and the red color deepened, while the rising steam seemed to pulse, almost like the beating of a heart.

"Eli, I need you to bend down and breathe in the steam as

deeply as you can," Whimsy said. "Then hold your breath until you feel as though you are being drawn toward the carving."

Eli leaned over the cauldron and drew in deep lungfuls of the steam, which smelled like herbs, tinged with a coppery tang and a hint of Arden's familiar, beloved scent. He kept breathing in, wanting more of Arden's scent—and suddenly he felt a strange pull, not as strong as the mate bond but just as inexorable.

"I feel it," he said, standing up straight. "I feel *him*."

Whimsy grinned. "It worked! Now we let you act like a big, furry compass and lead us right to him."

"Not so fast." Julian's voice held a note of caution. "We have to assume that wherever they've taken him, there's a possessed werewolf pack and the demon they summoned, and maybe the rest of Eli's pack, if they haven't all been possessed. We're going to need weapons, and I need to get that feather." He gave Eli an apologetic glance. "I know you probably want to go right now, but we'll only get one chance at this. We can't rush in unprepared. I've fought demons before, and it isn't easy."

"I don't want to do anything that might put Arden at risk," Eli said firmly. "We need to make a solid plan and have a backup plan too."

"Exactly." Julian nodded. He glanced at Tharn. "Are you up for this? We can use all the help we can get."

Tharn looked at Morag, then reached out and took her hand. "We're in. We said we'd help Eli get his pack back, and Arden's part of his pack now."

Earl and the others nodded, and Julian seemed pleased. "All right. I need to go back to my house. The feather is there, but I also have weapons. I'm glad we got all that holy water to cleanse the glyph—I have a feeling we're going to need it."

"Then let's go," Eli said, looking around at the others—his

comrades in arms. His friends now too. He'd come to Asheville to seek help from Tharn, and he'd found so much more. Together, they would find Arden, rescue Eli's pack, and free as many of the possessed werewolves as they could. The rest… well, if they couldn't be freed of the demon, they would have to be put down. He didn't want to kill his own kind, but if they threatened Arden, he wouldn't hesitate to strike the killing blow himself.

He wanted his mate, and God help anyone who stood in his way.

CHAPTER 14

rden didn't know where he was exactly, except in a whole lot of trouble.

When the possessed werewolves had attacked him in the forest, he'd been caught completely flat-footed. In retrospect, he should have been paying more attention to his surroundings, but he honestly hadn't considered the possibility that they'd come after him. He'd been far more worried that they'd want Eli, since Eli was the real danger to their plans. Arden wasn't exactly what anyone could consider much of a threat, especially not a bunch of strong supernaturals with a demon on their side.

Maybe they thought they could use him to get to Eli, but he wasn't about to cooperate and give them any information, no matter what they did to him. He would protect Eli with his own life, although he wasn't certain they had any way to know that. But until they decided to actually talk to him, he was in the figurative as well as the literal dark.

The werewolves hadn't wasted many words on him, and he wasn't certain if that was a good thing or a very bad one. They'd seemed to enjoy toying with him in the woods, growling and snapping at him as they'd tightened around him in a circle. He'd thought they were going to kill him, and he'd been more frightened than he'd ever been in his life.

But they hadn't hurt him, or not very much. One of them, the biggest, had clouted him with a massive paw and knocked him unconscious, but that had been the extent of it. He'd done more damage to himself, scraping his hands when he'd made a futile attempt to climb a tree to get away from them. If he'd noticed them sooner, he might have stood a chance, but by the time he became aware of their presence he hadn't had a chance. He'd been stupid, and now he was going to pay the price. Unless he could figure out a way to escape, he was never going to see Eli again.

When he'd regained his senses, Arden had quickly discovered he was bound with his hands behind his back and his ankles tied together. There was also some kind of dark sack over his head, which made it hard to breathe and impossible to see. From what he could tell, he was lying on a hard wooden floor, but he had no way of knowing where he'd been taken. He could be still in the Asheville area or hundreds of miles away.

But the most horrifying thing of all was that he couldn't feel the bond with Eli any longer. The special place inside him that had so recently been filled with Eli's warm presence was cold and empty. They'd likely taken him to someplace heavily warded by the demon, or maybe they'd possessed a wizard or witch who'd thrown the spell. Either way, Arden ached with loss, and he had no doubt Eli was frantic with worry. But since they'd had little luck in trying to find the pack before, he didn't think they were going to be able to find him either. Especially without the bond.

There also was no way of telling how much time had passed. He was thirsty, but that didn't tell him much. Still, he refused to give up without a fight, without making some effort, no matter how futile. He had too much to live for to accept being killed—or worse—at the hands of his captors. Though he had to admit, the "or worse" was the really terrifying part.

His wrists were tied together, but Arden was both small and agile. He drew in a deep breath, forcing himself to relax, then began to twist his arms against the restraints, grunting with the effort.

"That ain't gonna help, you know. We tried."

It was a woman's voice, and Arden went still. He'd thought he was alone, and not being able to see was suddenly a far greater handicap than he'd realized. But the voice wasn't mean or taunting; the soft, Southern drawl seeming to hold a hint of dry amusement.

"I'm at a bit of a disadvantage," Arden replied quietly. "Since I can't see, I didn't even know you were there."

"Yeah, they must be pretty pissed at you," another voice, this one male, added. "They was muttering something about what a real good show you was gonna be tonight."

Arden shuddered in reaction; he really didn't like how that sounded. He had a very good imagination, and the thoughts of what a "good show" would be for a bunch of possessed werewolves was the stuff of nightmares.

"Well, then, I guess I'm going to have to do whatever I can to disappoint them," he replied, keeping his tone light. "I'm going to take a wild guess here and assume that you're Eli's missing pack. Or what's left of it."

There was silence for several moments, and then the woman spoke again. "Yeah, that would be us. How do you know that?" There was an edge of suspicion in her voice, and all things considered, Arden couldn't really blame her.

"Because Eli came to Asheville to get help to find and rescue you. I'm part of the help. And also his mate."

"*Mate?*" Arden heard more than one gasp of astonishment,

then the woman hushed the others. "You expect us to believe Eli found his mate and let you out of his sight long enough for you to get snatched?"

"Well, it's not like either of us was exactly given a choice," Arden replied dryly. "Look... I think you're close to me, right? If I can get over to you, could you get this damned hood off?"

"I can try. If you take a couple of rolls in this direction, I'll see if there's anything I can do."

Arden did as instructed, then used his feet to push himself along the floor like an inchworm, following the woman's instructions. After several minutes, Arden felt her grip the hood, and she tugged at it until at last it came free.

He gulped in deep breaths of cool air, glancing around to take stock of his situation. The room they were in was of old, unpainted wood, high-ceilinged, and smelled faintly of hay and animals. Probably part of a barn, though from the age of the boards and the tinge of decay, it didn't seem to have been used in a long time.

He counted thirteen others—seven women and six men—in the room besides himself and the woman who had helped him. They were all bound much as he was, though their leg restraints had been tied to metal rings in the floor, separating them from each other, probably to keep them from helping one another get free. He looked at the woman, who was a pretty, sturdy-looking brunette with chin-length hair and wide blue eyes.

"Thank you," he said, grateful to be able to breathe freely and, most of all, to see again. "I'm Arden Gilmarin, by the way. Eli's mate."

"An *elf*?" The woman stared at him, then chuckled and shook her head. "No wonder he never found you. I would've loved to have seen his face when he realized he was bound to a teeny thing like you." The others seemed to share her amusement, if the snickers he heard were any indication.

"Yeah, it was a surprise for us both," Arden said. If they were all really lucky, maybe one day they'd get to swap stories about Eli's reaction to being mated to an elf, but now wasn't the time. "What's your name?"

"I'm Maggie White," the woman said. "I'd say 'pleased to meet you,' but that ain't exactly true. Not in these circumstances."

"I understand." Arden sighed, wondering if all werewolves had a gift for understatement. "There were nineteen of you taken… I guess the other five have been possessed?"

"You know that much?" Maggie's eyes widened, but then she grimaced. "Yeah. They were pulled out and taken to that demon. They started with the ones they figured looked the toughest. They were takin' us a couple at a time, but then they stopped yesterday. They left us alone until they threw you in here."

"That must have been when we erased the glyph." Arden nodded in satisfaction; at least they'd accomplished that much. "Eli and I and some friends of mine found George's body. We dealt with it, and it probably weakened the demon, just like we hoped. We were trying to figure out where you'd been taken when they tracked me down and brought me here."

For the first time, Maggie looked hopeful. "Eli won't stop until he finds you. He won't be able to, because the bond won't let him."

Arden winced. "There's just one problem with that—I can't feel him anymore. They must have magical wards on this place that block it." He hated to burst her bubble, but he felt he had to be truthful. "Unless he can somehow track me without it, I don't see how he can find us."

"Eli will find a way. He was looking for us when he found

you, right?" Maggie didn't seem as defeated as he would have thought, and he had to admire her spirit. "If the demon is weakened to where it can't possess any more of us, all we have to do is hold on until he finds us. I never doubted he was looking for us."

"He's thought of little else." Arden smiled slightly. He hoped she was right and that Eli somehow managed to find them all before it was too late.

He rolled up until he was in a sitting position behind Maggie, looking down at her bonds and wondering if he could somehow manage to free her hands. She glanced back over her shoulder, catching his eye and giving a slight nod, so he scooted until they were back to back, and he began to work at trying to loosen her bonds.

"Tell us how Eli found you," Maggie said, and so Arden started talking, finding the distraction welcome; it was better than sitting there doing nothing and fretting about what was going to happen. He began with Eli coming to the council, leaving out nothing, not even how Eli had wanted to put off any talk of taking Arden as his mate until after his pack had been found, but how the pull between them had been too strong in the end.

"That's how it is," Maggie said quietly. "You can't resist it."

"No, I guess you're right," Arden replied. He hated the hollow ache he felt inside at the loss of his bond to Eli. Even if it had only been a day since it had been fully formed, it had already become a part of him.

"I don't know if this magic they've got that's suppressing our bonds is a good thing or a bad thing," she continued, and he could almost feel the pain in her words. "My mate, Steven, is one of the ones they took, day before yesterday. If he's possessed, it would probably make this even harder to take."

The very thought made Arden shiver. "I can believe it."

He'd continued working on her bonds, trying to loosen

the tight knots. The faint light that was coming in through the high windows began to dim, and he knew it must be getting close to sunset. Eli was probably frantic by now, and Arden wished he could do something—anything—that might help his mate find them.

The knots he'd been pulling at suddenly slackened, and he went still. "I think…."

He didn't get to complete the sentence. The door was abruptly pushed open, and two big men entered the room. They didn't even glance at the other prisoners, coming straight to Arden.

These were part of the possessed pack, Arden had no doubt. He saw the pulsing black of their auras, the same thing he'd noticed when the wolves had attacked him in the forest. One of them, a mean-looking bruiser of a man with an ugly scar down his left cheek, grabbed Arden by one arm and yanked him painfully up.

"Your turn, pointy ears," he growled. "You've been a bad boy, and now you're gonna get what's coming to you."

An electric jolt of fear went through Arden, but there was nothing he could do except glance back at Maggie. She met his gaze, then nodded to him. He hoped it meant that she'd managed to work her hands free, because from the sound of it, she might be the only one who could help him.

He was dragged roughly from the room, out into a larger, open area. He saw that he'd been right about the structure being a barn, and the pack was being held in what must have once been a supply room. Now he was in the central part of the structure, with the ceiling rising up almost thirty feet overhead. There were haylofts up under the eaves, but what got his attention were the twenty or so people standing around him in a rough circle. Harsh white light shone down from overhead fluorescent lamps, but he didn't think the stark shadows on the faces of the gathered werewolves were the only reason they looked menacing.

He didn't know what was going to happen, but whatever it was, Arden knew he had to stall for time if he could. "Hey, y'all," he drawled in an exaggerated accent, pinning a bright, false smile on his face. "Did all of you come here just to see me? Really? I'm flattered."

"Shut up!" The werewolf who'd been holding Arden's arm suddenly released him, then backhanded him hard across the mouth.

Pain burst through his head, and Arden fell heavily to the dirt floor, stunned from the force of the blow. Stars swam across his vision, and he shook his head, trying to clear it. "No need to be rude," he muttered, watching as the werewolf stalked away to join the circle. "It's not sporting to hit someone who can't fight back."

The werewolf didn't reply, but Arden was suddenly distracted by the way the air around him began to grow cold. It was as though someone had opened the door to a freezer, and icy fingers were reaching out to wrap themselves around him. Then he began to feel the same sensation he'd experienced in the woods when he'd gotten close to the settlement of George's pack—a sense of wrongness that made his heart begin to pound hard.

The light in the room dimmed suddenly, and Arden looked up. Something like a dark fog had gathered beneath the lights, seeming to bend and twist in on itself. A wave of nausea rose in him, because he knew what he was seeing. The demon that had been summoned was manifesting.

He couldn't look away, watching in numb horror as the darkness descended to the floor only a few feet in front of him. It coalesced slowly, and Arden hoped it was because it was weaker without the glyph to draw upon. But weakened or not, it took physical form, appearing at last as a two-legged creature almost ten feet tall, with skin the color of ash and eyes that burned like two fiery coals in a horned, misshapen head. Its mouth was a lipless gash full of spiked teeth, and it radiated waves of cold, malevolent energy. The ugliness of its aura made bile rise in the back of Arden's throat, and he knew without a doubt that he was looking at a creature of pure, concentrated evil.

"You!" Its voice was like the scratching of nails on a chalkboard. "You're the one who destroyed my glyph!"

A part of Arden wanted to curl into a ball and die rather than face this thing, but he summoned up all his courage. Maybe the thing didn't know about Eli and the others, focusing on Arden because he'd been the one who'd used the feather, and Arden wasn't about to call its attention to his mate and his friends. He didn't know what he could do to protect them, but he was going to try.

"Guilty," he replied. "I figured that might piss you off."

A growl rose from the gathered werewolves, and the demon snarled, seeming to peer at him closely. "You're no demon hunter! Where is he? It was no puny elf who banished my glyph! I felt the angelic presence that broke it. Where is he? Tell me!"

Arden grimaced, feeling a surge of bitter anger at Micah Carter. If the old man had been the one dealing with the glyph, he might have banished the demon entirely, and then Arden wouldn't be in this mess. But it might have only focused the demon's anger on Micah, and Arden wasn't the kind of person who could wish this on anyone, no matter what they'd done. He also wasn't going to give the demon the old man's name, no matter what it did to him.

"Sorry, it really was me," Arden replied. He didn't know if demons could detect lies as angels were supposed to be able to do, and in this case he certainly hoped so. "Why do people constantly underestimate me? I'm going to end up with a complex."

The demon shrieked, and Arden felt a certain satisfaction in having stood his ground. But the feeling was short-lived.

"Very well, then, elf! You're no angel-spawn, but you're pure enough to do."

It gestured with a clawed hand, and two of the werewolves left the circle, coming toward Arden. His bravado quickly turned to alarm as they grabbed his arms and hauled him up. One of them grabbed his hair, yanking Arden's head back and sending a jolt of pain through him. Eyes wide, he watched the demon approach.

"Since you're so proud to have destroyed my glyph, I'm going to use you to make it again," the demon hissed. "You creatures are fond of justice, aren't you? How do you like mine?"

Arden didn't like it at all, but he was also powerless to stop it. He'd never felt so helpless in his life, and as he stared up into the demon's fiery eyes, all he could think about was Eli. He hoped that his death wasn't going to hurt his mate and that Eli would forgive him for having gotten himself captured and killed. And that Eli didn't do anything to get himself hurt by seeking vengeance.

Closing his eyes, he pictured Eli's beautiful face, wanting that to be the last thing he saw before he died, not the visage of the demon. He held on to the image of Eli as he looked that morning, warm and sleepy and sated from a night spent in discovering the pleasure they could give one another.

He could feel the foul presence of the demon drawing closer, felt the cold enveloping him, numbing his skin like ice. Drawing in a last breath, Arden whispered Eli's name.

That was when all hell broke loose.

The demon shrieked, and Arden fell to the ground as his captors dropped him. He opened his eyes, watching in disbelief as the circle of werewolves suddenly broke into clusters of men and wolves fighting one another. There were far more bodies than there had been, and he thought at first that Maggie must have released the others of her pack and that they'd attacked. But then he caught sight of Eli running toward him, and he realized that his mate had come to save him.

Eli had partially transformed into a creature that was a hybrid of wolf and man with bared fangs and sharp claws already dripping with blood. Somehow he looked even bigger, and his eyes blazed with fury. But he moved with purpose and control, the rational mind of the man appearing ascendant over the mindless rage of the wolf as he bore down on the demon that had threatened Arden.

An icy fist of dread wrapped around Arden's heart as he watched Eli spring upon the demon, but Eli's attack was calculated. He landed on the demon's back, and the evil creature gave an unearthly scream as Eli raised his arm, then brought it down over the demon's shoulder and rammed a wicked-looking dagger through the demon's chest, where the heart would be had it been human. It was a blow that would have felled any mortal creature, but the demon remained upright and grabbed at Eli with razor-sharp claws.

Eli seemed to expect the move, because he released his hold on the demon, dropping to the ground and rolling between its legs to avoid the attack. Eli was fast, coming to his feet before the demon could turn back to face him. He used the dagger again, thrusting it up through the demon's abdomen, twisting the blade and ripping it back to slice open the flesh. This made the demon howl in rage and pain, and Arden realized that in manifesting in a physical form, the demon seemed to have made itself vulnerable to weapons.

As Eli dodged away from the demon's claws once more, Arden caught sight of two of the possessed werewolves heading toward him, obviously intent on protecting their master. He opened his mouth to cry out a warning, but before he could even draw breath, there was a blur of movement, and he watched as Maggie and the other werewolves from Eli's pack dashed across the room, transforming as they moved. They slammed into the possessed werewolves, snarling and ripping at their former captors with teeth and claws.

Eli had paid no attention to the attempted flanking maneuver, never taking his eyes off his real opponent. The demon swiped at him and managed to catch Eli's left arm with a claw, shredding the sleeve of his leather jacket. Red blood welled up, and Arden thrashed in helpless fury at seeing his mate wounded. He'd never been a violent person, but the sight of Eli's blood made him want to attack the demon with his bare hands and tear it apart.

Unfortunately there was nothing he could do except watch helplessly as Eli backed warily away. The demon hissed in satisfaction, seeming to gather itself for a rushing attack, but Eli was obviously an experienced fighter. A moment before the demon sprang, Eli was moving, rushing in under its arms to thrust the dagger up into the open wound, driving it in so hard and deep that the blade was lodged fast.

"Mortal fool!" The demon seemed slower and weaker, but it was still a formidable opponent, and Eli was now unarmed except for his own claws. Eli stood between Arden and the demon, backing toward Arden as the demon stepped forward, obviously intent on ripping Eli apart.

Suddenly a bolt flew out of the shadows to the left, impacting the demon in the head. Startled, Arden glanced in that direction, seeing Julian lower the arm he had used to fire the crossbow. Julian looked grimly satisfied, and he raised his other hand in an obscene gesture at the demon.

Arden's attention had been drawn from Eli, and apparently so had the demon's. But rather than pressing an attack or running away, Eli had used the diversion to unzip his jacket and reach inside. As Arden's gaze returned to his mate, he saw a blaze of white light surrounding Eli, as he raised his arm, holding up the angel feather. Before the demon could react, Eli rushed forward, using the feather like a weapon and thrusting it through the demon's body.

There was a scream, but it wasn't something Arden heard with his ears. It was on a different level, a shriek of pure, unfettered rage. The demon burst into blue flame, consumed in an instant and leaving nothing but a final blast of cold air behind.

Eli rushed over to Arden, transforming completely back into his human form with each step. "Are you hurt?" he asked as he knelt beside Arden and ran his hands along Arden's arms and legs as if checking for injuries.

When the demon disappeared, it seemed to have taken the wards with it, because Arden could feel Eli again, and he almost wept in relief. He could sense Eli's worry, and he shook his head, swallowing past a lump in his throat before he could speak. "No, I'm fine now. You're the one who's hurt!"

"We're tough, and we heal right fast. I'll be fine," Eli said. He tore off the ropes that bound Arden, the muscles in his arms bulging as he used his enhanced strength. As soon as Arden was free, Eli pulled him into a tight embrace.

Arden wrapped his arms around Eli, holding on to him tightly. He'd been so certain he was going to die, that he'd never see Eli again, that he couldn't hold back tears of happiness. "You saved me," he murmured. "My hero. My Eli."

Eli sat down and drew Arden into his lap, rubbing Arden's back as he rocked back and forth. "My Arden," he said, a soft growl underlying his voice. "You scared the hell outta me, getting yourself snatched like that."

"I didn't mean to," Arden replied. He sniffled, wiping at his eyes with one hand. "I don't know how they found me."

"It must have been when you erased the glyph." Julian stepped up behind Eli, and Arden saw relief on his friend's face.

Arden frowned. "I wonder if I did it wrong."

Julian shrugged, then shook his head. "I don't think so. I guess the demon got some kind of psychic lock on you when the glyph fell. Maybe that's one reason Micah didn't want to do it himself and risk being attacked." He scowled. "I'm going to have words with him."

"What about the rest of our pack, and the survivors of George's?" Maggie approached them, her expression tight. "They were all knocked senseless when the demon disappeared. We're getting them tied up, but… what can we do with them?"

"The feather?" Eli gave Julian a questioning look. "It'll take a while to get to all of them with it disappearing back to the box every time, but it's worth a try, ain't it?"

"Yes, of course," Julian replied. "Maybe we can use it on more than one at a time, especially for the ones that haven't been possessed for very long. I don't hold out much hope for the ones from the original pack, though. Especially the ones that have been possessed for years. But we should do it while we're here, since Whimsy and the witches threw a purification circle around the building. None of the possessed ones will be able to escape."

"Then we'll have to put them down," Eli said, his voice quiet and tinged with regret. "Give me a minute, and I'll help. I just—"

"Arden!" A joyous cry cut off whatever Eli intended to say, and Arden looked up to see Whimsy running to him.

Whimsy knelt beside Arden and flung his arms around his shoulders. "I'm so glad you're okay!"

Arden laughed, wrapping one arm around Whimsy and returning the embrace. "I'm glad too, believe me! Thanks for coming to my rescue." He looked at Julian, and then at Eli. "All of you."

Julian snorted. "We've gotten used to your fussing, brat. We'd just have to break in another hovery half-elf, and that's a lot of work," he said, but his voice held affection.

"It was a group effort," Eli said, glancing around at the others with obvious gratitude. "Tharn and his pack helped. So did Brianna and her coven. Now we just gotta clean up the mess. But me and Arden need a minute," he added, the authoritative note in his voice making it clear he wasn't making a request.

"Sure thing." Whimsy kissed Arden's cheek and then stood up and went to Julian, reaching for his hand. Julian took it, then pulled Whimsy close and put an arm over his shoulders as they walked away.

Maggie nodded and turned away, and Arden smiled, reaching up to lay his hand against Eli's cheek. "I like it when you go all alpha," he said. "It's sexy."

Eli smiled slightly as he leaned into the touch, but his gaze was pensive. "I couldn't feel you," he said, tapping his chest. "It was the worst thing I've ever felt in my life. Worse than coming home after my pack was taken."

"I know what you mean." Arden stroked Eli's cheek. "I felt like part of me had been ripped away."

"Me too." Eli turned his head and pressed a kiss to Arden's palm. "But it taught me something. You done built yourself a little nest in my heart, and it'll be yours for as long as I live."

Arden felt himself in danger of melting into a ball of goo. "Really?" he smiled. "Do you mind it?"

"Naw, you're my mate," Eli said, giving Arden a squeeze. "You're part of me now. I felt what it'd be like if I lost you. I don't never want to feel it again."

"Neither do I," Arden replied fervently, and then he chuckled. "We've known each other what… four days? And I know I can't live without you. I love you, Eli."

"It's crazy, but it feels right and true." Eli caught Arden's chin and drew him into a light but lingering kiss. "I love you too, Itty Bitty."

Closing his eyes, Arden savored the kiss, pushing his hand into Eli's hair and feeling the strands twine around his fingers, just as Eli had twined himself around his heart. He'd been kidnapped and very nearly sacrificed by a demon, and they still had unpleasant issues to deal with. But for the moment, he let himself indulge in one perfect moment. He was safe, he was happy, and for Eli's love, he'd gladly take on even hell itself.

CHAPTER 15

$\mathcal{E}$li stood on a small dais at the far end of the common hall at Tharn's settlement with Tharn on one side and Arden on the other. Maggie, Eli's second-in-command, stood nearby as they prepared to address a gathering of Tharn's pack, Eli's pack, and the survivors from George's pack.

There weren't many. Even the feather hadn't been able to bring some of the possessed werewolves back, and those who did recover reported that the strongest fighters—the ones who had likely been possessed the longest—had left before the night that Arden was going to be sacrificed. The survivors didn't know why they left or where they were going, and Eli didn't like knowing there were still demon-possessed werewolves on the loose, even if there were only a handful. Fortunately, Tharn had been as good as his word, so every pack within a hundred miles knew to be on guard, and both Tharn and Eli intended to make sure the news would spread even farther. The demons would have a much harder time finding victims now.

But tonight they were gathered to handle other matters.

Eli had made some decisions, things he hadn't even discussed with Arden yet, but he was content with his plans for the future.

"We've called you here tonight to lay out your options," Eli said, sweeping his gaze across the crowd. "As y'all know, I found my mate." He slid his arm around Arden's shoulders, proud to show off his mate to the other werewolves—especially Earl. "He's a respected businessman here in Asheville, and his people are here too, so I've decided to move to Asheville to be with him."

A murmur of surprise rippled through the crowd, but none of the werewolves raised any objection, and Tharn clapped Eli on the shoulder in a show of support.

Arden nestled close, wrapping his arms around Eli's waist. He gazed up at Eli, his green eyes soft with affection. "Are you sure you want to move?" he asked quietly. "I don't want you to give up your home for me."

"Clayton's just a place," Eli said, stroking Arden's back. "You're my home."

Arden smiled, then tightened his arms around Eli in a fierce hug. "And you're mine. Always."

"Damn right," Eli said, and then he turned his attention back to the werewolves. "Anyone who don't want to go back to Georgia can stay here with me as part of a new pack. If you don't want me as your alpha, there's room in Tharn's pack. If you wanna go back to Georgia, you can go with Maggie. She's taking over my pack with my blessing. Anyone who don't like that can take it up with her," he said, grinning as Maggie bared her teeth in a fierce display.

Maggie had earned her place in Eli's pack with her strength and her levelheadedness, proving to be a worthy fighter and a trusted advisor. Eli had no qualms about leaving his pack in her capable hands, and he had no doubt she would successfully defend her position if she had to.

"You don't have to decide tonight, but Maggie's going back to Clayton in three days' time," Eli continued. "You wanna go, you see her before then. You wanna stay, you see me or Tharn. I'll give you my phone number tonight if you want it."

He had a brand new smartphone now thanks to Arden, who'd talked him into it by telling him all about the naughty potential in video chatting. He'd also moved into Arden's treehouse, and he'd been talking to a couple of Tharn's pack mates who worked as park rangers about a job. He'd been a park ranger in Georgia, and he thought it might be easy enough to transfer to the Great Smoky Mountains National Park, especially if he had someone on the inside vouching for him.

"If you got any questions, we'll be walking around," Eli said, and then he turned to Tharn. "Anything you wanna say?"

"Only that any that want to join me will be welcome," Tharn said. "And I think it should be obvious that all three packs can now claim kin with one another, so I expect all of y'all to help out with giving Eli here a proper send-off when he and Arden get hitched."

Arden laughed, and the tips of his ears turned pink. "If there are buff strippers involved, I'm going to have to insist on being invited!"

Eli raised one eyebrow at Tharn. He hadn't thought about anything beyond the mate bond, which was far deeper and more binding than a marriage, but now that Tharn had put the idea in his head, he realized he liked the idea of having a ring on Arden's finger as well.

"You're getting a little ahead of me. I ain't even asked him yet, but now that you mention it...." Eli went down on one knee in front of Arden and clasped Arden's hand. "Will you do me the honor of being my husband as well as my mate?"

Arden squeezed Eli's fingers, and for a moment he pretended to consider the question. But he couldn't keep from smiling and finally gave up any pretense. "Yes! Yes, of course!"

"Brat," Eli growled, but he kissed Arden's palm before climbing to his feet. "Well, I reckon we got ourselves a reason to celebrate tonight too."

"I feel like I have a reason to celebrate every night," Arden said softly. "I get to sleep beside the man I love—that's the best present I've ever gotten."

"Me too," Eli said, drawing Arden into his arms and holding him close.

Scarcely a week before, Eli thought he was on the verge of losing everything, but he had gained far more than he ever imagined possible. He had no regrets about his decision to stay. Arden had far more roots in Asheville than Eli had in Clayton, and he would be satisfied as long as he had a pack to call his own, no matter how big or small.

As long as he had Arden, his heart had its home.

ABOUT THE AUTHOR

Rachel Langella and Ari McKay are the professional pseudonyms for Arionrhod and McKay, who have been writing together for over a decade. Their collaborations encompass a wide variety of romance genres, including contemporary, fantasy, science fiction, gothic, and action/adventure. Their work includes the Blood Bathory series of paranormal novels, the Herc's Mercs series, as well as two historical Westerns: *Heart of Stone* and *Finding Forgiveness*. When not writing, they can often be found scheming over costume designs or binge watching TV shows together.

Ari McKay is a retired systems engineer turned full-time writer and seamstress. Now that she is an empty-nester, she has turned her attentions to finding the perfect piece of land to build a fortress in preparation for the zombie apocalypse, and baking (and eating) far too many cakes.

Rachel Langella is a creative writing teacher who has been writing for one reason or another most of her life. She loves all things spooky and/or vintage, and she's given in to Ari's corruptive influences and learned to sew so she can make her own vintage-style clothes and costumes. Given she has the survival skills of a gnat, she's relying on Ari to help her survive the zombie apocalypse.

Visit Rachel and Ari on:
Website: arimckay.com

Facebook:

https://www.facebook.com/ari.mckay.7
And
https://www.facebook.com/rachel.langella.9

Twitter:
@AriMcKay1
And
@LangellaRachel

ALSO BY RACHEL LANGELLA

ASHEVILLE ARCANA

Out of the Ashes

Fate works in mysterious—and dangerous—ways.

Alpha werewolf Eli Hammond returns from a fishing trip to discover five members of his pack have been murdered and the rest are missing. He needs help and he needs it fast. His one hope lies with the supernatural council in Asheville, North Carolina, but they turn their backs on him.

Except for Arden Gilmarin.

Eli is stunned—and not especially thrilled—to discover half-elf Arden is his destined mate. But as Arden and his friends, Whimsy and Julian, help with his quest to find his pack, Eli surrenders to the demands of his wolf—and his heart. They'll need to bond together, because the evil that stole Eli's pack now has its sights set on Arden. If Eli wants to save his mate and his pack, he's in for the fight of his life.

Forged In Fire

For three hundred years, Harlan Edgewood's monthly shifts have been agonizing. Then he meets Whimsy Hickes—a mage who specializes in transformation—and the attraction is both immediate and mutual. But Harlan takes refuge in denial, believing his curse is too great a burden to inflict on any lover.

But Whimsy knows he can help.

When Harlan is provoked into an unexpected transformation,
Whimsy uses his magic to ease Harlan's pain, but with an
unexpected consequence. While he's shifted, Harlan's wolf
recognizes Whimsy as his mate.

Yet even as they try to figure out their relationship given Harlan's
doubts, suspicious events in the Asheville magical community
escalate. Shifters are disappearing, others are murdered, and
Harlan's curse makes him an obvious target. It will take all of
Whimsy's magic to drive back the rising evil—and if he fails, Harlan
will lose not only his life, but his very soul.

Quenched In Blood

Vampire Julian Schaden warned the Asheville Paranormal Council
of an impending demonic incursion for decades. Over the past two
years, he and his friends have fought hard with little help because
Micah Carter, the demon hunter who should have led them,
abandoned his responsibilities long before his death.

In desperation, Julian visits the Carter property and finds a miracle:
Thomas Carter, heir to a long line of demon hunters. Thomas
knows nothing about the supernatural world, but the prospect of a
real life outside the sheltered, isolated farm calls to him, and the
idea of fighting the Unholy feels right.

Thomas is too young and innocent for Julian, but opposites attract,
and this is one battle Julian seems fated to lose. But a prophecy
from a dying mage comes with a bleak warning: the upcoming
battle will claim Thomas's life. To keep the world safe, Julian may
have to sacrifice the only love he's ever known.

9 798227 930347